Dear Canada

A Ribbon of
Shining Steel

∽∾

The Railway Diary of
Kate Cameron

BY JULIE LAWSON

Scholastic Canada Ltd.

Yale, British Columbia,
Dominion of Canada,
1882

Monday, August 28, 1882, 7 P.M.

Hell's Gate and Galoshes! I am well pleased today — and thankful for God's tender mercies. After the events of yesterday, I might not have *had* a today.

This is what happened. I was spending the week's end at Rachel's farm in Spuzzum and Rachel came up with a daring idea. We would follow the Wagon Road to a spot near the Alexandra Suspension Bridge where her brothers keep their boat, then we would borrow the boat and float a short distance downriver. And we did!

The Fraser was low and everything was fine at first, but it was a wild stretch of water and it was not long before we panicked and decided to end the Adventure. We steered the boat to shore — with great difficulty — and Rachel jumped out with rope in hand. The plan was for me to jump out as well and together we would pull the boat back to its hiding place and return to Rachel's farm before anyone was the wiser. But Great Godfrey, before I had a chance to jump out, the current dragged the rope out of Rachel's hands and I was adrift and flying down the Canyon.

The river was swift and muddy — boiling with spray and seething with treacherous whirlpools —

but in spite of my terror I noticed a large flat rock a few feet from shore. I took hold of the rope and with heart in hands leapt out upon the rock, waded to shore, tied the boat to a tree and climbed the rocky bluff, goodness knows how.

I ended up at a roadhouse — wet and shaky, fingers scraped and bleeding, clothing fair torn to shreds — and lo and behold, there was the Express pulling out. Mr. Tingley stopped his team, wrapped me in a rug and tucked me inside the coach. A kind passenger gave me a sip of brandy from his flask.

Mr. Tingley cracked his whip and the horses raced off toward Spuzzum. On the way we passed Rachel and her parents and brothers, anxiously out looking for me. Poor Rachel was in Hysterics, certain I had drowned. But here I am, safe and sound.

So that is why I am *exceedingly* thankful. Mama and Papa are thankful, too, for they have presented me with this Diary. It even has a ribbon to mark my place. Papa told me if I want to grow up and be a newspaper reporter like Mr. Hagan (which I do), I had better start practising. He said, "Keep your wits about you and your eyes and ears open."

Toby said I had better hide the Diary when *he's* around because his eyes and ears are open, too. Andrew failed to show the slightest interest, being otherwise engaged in oiling his new rifle. He showed a considerable amount of interest in my Ad-

4

venture, however. He even showed Admiration for my courage and pluck. But not openly, of course, being Andrew.

Mama told me that she kept a Diary when she was a girl. She said I could record my Private Thoughts and Feelings as well as the things I see and hear — and *survive*. She also said I must exercise more caution in the future, especially when gallivanting with Rachel. I promised her I would.

Papa told me I should use my Diary to record "lessons learned," beginning with my foray on the river.

Here is my first LESSON LEARNED: Next time I will be the *first* to leap out of the boat.

Same Day, 9 P.M.

In case anyone dares to read my Diary (warning: Toby), "Hell's Gate" is not a blasphemy even tho' it contains the word H___. It is a real place on the Canyon so I can say it.

Tuesday, August 29

All day long Toby pestered me with questions about my Adventure, hoping to catch me out in a lie. How fast was the river flowing? How big were the rapids? How slippery was the rock? How far from shore? He says I was carried away by words more than by river. He says no one could have survived.

Well, Simon Fraser did when he was exploring the river in the first place. And I did, too. I confess I may have exaggerated a little. But only in the telling. My *written* account is the Honest Truth.

Toby's final question: How did the brandy taste?

Awful! So he needn't be jealous. Brandy tastes much better when it is hidden in plum pudding.

Friday, September 1, 8 P.M.

I could spit nails. Serves me right, listening at doors, but Hell's Gate, hearing the words *Kate, wild, college* and *lady* — all in the same sentence — compelled me to listen.

Now the cat is out of the bag. My parents are plotting to send me away to VICTORIA. To a school for Anglican girls called Angela College where they trust I will learn the necessary Social Graces. Necessary for what? Blasts and brimstones! I wanted to storm into the parlour and bellow, "Yale has social graces! Why can't I stay here?"

And what of my brothers? They are the ones lacking in graces, social and otherwise.

I also heard Mama say what a pity they cannot afford to send me to school in England *after all*. Aha! They have been hatching this plot for some time. Only one thing to do. Hatch a plot of my own.

Same Day, 9 P.M.

Here is my plan.

I, Kathleen Louise Cameron, born in Toronto, Canada, on February 15, 1870, hereby pledge to do the following:

1. Act in a gracious, ladylike manner so that Mama will no longer think Angela College is necessary.

2. Go through all the magazines that Grandma Forrest sends from England and re-read every article that pertains to Social Graces.

3. Refrain from moving quickly, speaking loudly and talking too much in an overly exuberant manner.

4. Walk with a book on my head to improve my posture.

Naturally this pledge does not apply to my Diary. Within these pages I can be my un-refrained self. The same when I am with Rachel.

Pledge #3 will be a torture. Especially tomorrow, because it is going to be an exciting day. Mr. Onderdonk has arranged for a locomotive to push five flatcars up the Canyon so everyone can watch the *Skuzzy* go through Hell's Gate.

Saturday, September 2

Hip, hip for the *Skuzzy*! That's what we thought first thing this morning. Now we are home and no-one's hip-hipping anymore.

Off we went, dressed in our Sunday best to mark the occasion — along with half the town. That *Skuzzy*! It has been months since she first tried to get through Hell's Gate — without succeeding — and everyone was convinced that *this* time she would make it. "Won't it be grand!" everyone said. Because then the supplies that Mr. Onderdonk needs to build the railway can go by river instead of by the Wagon Road and it won't cost Mr. O. so much money.

Not that I care two figs.

Fine morning — blue and purple mountains over the trees across the river — and lots of time to admire the view. We stood on the cliff at Hell's Gate and watched and watched and waited and waited. Poor little *Skuzzy*! Smoke and steam gushed out of her smokestack and her boiler must have been fit to burst. She strained and struggled and tried so hard, but the rapids kept pushing her back. After five hours, we gave up and came home. Other people stayed and kept watching.

The best part was riding on the cars. The tracks going north up the Canyon are newly laid and we were the first passengers to try them out.

Even though the *Skuzzy* failed in her attempt, I believe I succeeded in mine. I stood quietly on the river bank instead of playing tag or gallivanting about with the other children. I did not raise my voice, not even on the train ride, where it was impossible to be heard otherwise. I was so quiet Papa asked what was wrong. And when we got home Mama complimented me on the way I had kept my Sunday best clean enough to wear to church tomorrow. I thanked her graciously.

Sunday, September 3

Church this A.M. Several empty pews because a lot of people are still at Hell's Gate watching the *Skuzzy*. Rev. Horlock should have preached a sermon on persistence. Maybe he did — I confess I was daydreaming instead of paying attention.

Spent the rest of the day reading and *trying* to put myself in a quiet Sunday mood. All I can think about is Back-to-School Tomorrow. I wish Rachel were going to be there.

Monday, September 4

New term at school. Same teacher as last year with the same bristly moustache and twitchy eyebrows. I watched closely all day long to see if he'd do his trick of raising one eyebrow and not the other. Alas, he didn't.

Everyone was lively after the holidays but Teacher said our brains are in sore need of a waking. He "cracked the whip" a number of times and rapped more than a few knuckles, including Rusty's.

For Penmanship we wrote:

Quidnuncs query with queer quizzical questions.

What are *Quidnuncs*? I wanted to ask Teacher but was afraid my knuckles would be rapped for being Impudent.

Impudent: cocky and bold.

I am going to keep track of tricky words and their meanings so I will do better in this year's Examination.

Tuesday, September 5

I learned but one thing today — a *quidnunc* is a busybody. And a very odd-looking word.

Wednesday, September 6

Thrilling news — a PRINCESS is coming to Yale and we have the same name. I asked everyone at home to call me Louise from now on. Mama gave me a funny look, until I reminded her that Louise is my middle name and sounds much more elegant than Kate. Thank goodness I've been practising my Social Graces, especially Comportment. Now I must learn to curtsey. And I must start walking with a heavier book on my head.

Princess Louise is the fourth daughter of Queen Victoria and she will be coming with her husband, the Governor General of Canada. They will be here early next month!

Saturday, September 9

Toby and Andrew went hunting without me. I am only pretending to mind since I do not much care for shooting game — only eating it — but they could have gone fishing instead, and taken me.

I have finished my chores, written letters to Grandma Forrest and Rachel — and even to Mary Beth in Ottawa, in spite of the fact she has not yet replied to the letter I wrote last June. The mail is slow, but not that slow.

With all that done, and nothing else to do, I am writing in my Diary.

SIGHTS AND SOUNDS:
Grey sky
Drizzle
Cottonwood tree
Crows: caw caw
Chickens: cluck
Railway: blast, bang, clank, rumble, blast

Mrs. Murray's dog: yap yap
Stern-wheeler: TOOT!
Me: sniff, sniff.

I must be coming down with a cold. *Do not let Mama know.* An ounce of cure is worse than a thousand pounds of anything.

THOUGHTS AND FEELINGS:

I suppose Mary Beth in Ottawa has forgotten me by now. It is a Trial being Best Friends when you are thousands of miles away.

Moving is a Trial.

Moving to Yale *was* a Trial, but now I like it here. I hope we never move again — unless it is upriver to Spuzzum.

If my parents send me to Angela College, I will run off and live in Rachel's barn with the horses.

Thank goodness for Mr. Hagan! When we first came to Yale he gave us a tour of his newspaper and I showed such an interest he said that I could drop by *any time* and learn the ins and outs of being a newspaper reporter. Now is a good time! I'm done with thoughts and feelings.

Sunday, September 10

The *Skuzzy* is still trying to get through Hell's Gate.

Monday, September 11

Mr. Hagan has a map on his wall so he can keep track of the railway progress. There is a lot of tracking to keep, with gangs working in different sections all through the Fraser Canyon — blasting tunnels, laying track, building bridges and so on. Papa is building the bridge at Skuzzy Creek, near Boston Bar, and when it's finished, Mr. Hagan says I can mark it on his map. Last year he let me draw the railway tracks between Emory and Yale when that section got finished, and he said I could draw in the tracks all the way to Boston Bar. But that part is taking a long time. Papa says it probably won't be finished for at least another year. And the total from Emory to Boston Bar is only 29 miles.

Wednesday, September 13

Why am I cursed with brothers? This is what horrid Toby said today — "I can see his brains, Kate! They're oozing all over the stretcher!"

My Pledge momentarily forgotten, I ran to the window. It was admittedly a gruesome sight, but I felt obliged to have a look so I could record the details in my Diary.

Alas, Mama was too quick. She yanked us away from the window and drew the curtains.

She is forever scolding Papa for buying a house so

close to Mr. Onderdonk's Accident Hospital. "The children know the railway work is dangerous," she tells him. "They do not need a constant reminder."

Mama often goes to help care for the accident victims. I would like to help, too, but Mama says I'm not old enough. Perhaps it is for the best. I may not be brave enough to withstand the sight of too much blood.

I wonder if a person can be a reporter and still have Social Graces. It must be important to act hastily at times, in order to capture an event as it unfolds. Is it possible to act both gracefully and hastily? I'm beginning to think not.

Thursday, September 14

Awake all night. It was my own fault — I should never have looked at that poor man going into the hospital because all it did was give me nightmares.

It was my usual nightmare — someone is being carried into the hospital on a stretcher and the blanket is pulled back and the face is so battered and bloodied from exploding rocks it is unrecognizable — but I know it is Papa.

Mama says we should be thankful he is building bridges and not blasting tunnels, since most of the accidents occur where there is blasting. But I have nightmares all the same. I could never help out in the Hospital. What was I thinking? I would never be able to sleep.

Friday, September 15

Finally! Finished schoolwork and dinner and after-dinner chores, and now I'm free to write about today — before it is completely over. So here it is, starting from this morning.

I woke to the sound of blasting, as usual. I wish I had been here to mark the occasion when the first big blast happened, back on May 15, 1880, about four months *before* we arrived in Yale. I do not care for the noise and vibrations, but it would have been something to see the first bit of granite blown out of the cliff to make the *First Railway Tunnel* north of Yale.

The blasting has been going on steadily ever since. You would think that after two years I would be used to it, but it still shakes the house and gives me a nasty jolt — even though it is happening farther up the line now.

A usual morning: tended the chickens, gathered the eggs, ate one for breakfast (egg, not chicken) and put aside two yolks for washing my hair this evening.

Then I walked to school with my brothers. Toby talked my ear off. I listened graciously, showing great interest in his tales, but he did not seem to notice, just kept on talking. Andrew was his normal quiet self, probably thinking about his next hunting trip. He brought home three grouse the other day and we had grouse for dinner.

At school we had Sketching, my favourite subject. And Geography. Teacher called on me to point out the location of Calcutta and I'm pleased to say I found it in short order. Unlike Rusty, who stares blankly at a world map and cannot even find his own continent. No wonder his knuckles get rapped.

After school I came home. And here I am. It wasn't much of a day.

I wish I'd had my Diary two years ago. I could have written all about our journey from Ontario to British Columbia. Mr. Hagan often describes his journeys up and down the railway line and prints them in the *Sentinel* for everyone to read. I could do the same, except that I've forgotten most of the details. Here is what I do remember —

We left Ottawa, Ontario, and took the Union Pacific Railroad across the United States of America, all the way to San Francisco. Papa kept telling us that one day we would be able to take a train across Canada — from sea to shining sea — thanks to him and Mr. Onderdonk and all the workers who are presently engaged in building the railway.

In San Francisco I had my first view of the ocean.

It is called the Pacific. Papa says the name comes from the Spanish word *pacifica*, which means calm, but it was not calm and when we got on the steamship and sailed to Victoria I was seasick the entire time. I do not know the Spanish word for *wretched* or *stormy* but that is what the ocean should have been called.

We arrived in Victoria and Papa went on to Yale to make preparations for our arrival. We stayed in a hotel. After a few days we left Victoria on a stern-wheeler and went across the Strait of Georgia to New Westminster. We spent one night there and the next day we got on another stern-wheeler, the *Western Slope*, that went up the Fraser River to Yale.

I remember holding my breath in awe as we ploughed up the mighty Fraser, hemmed in by high wooded hills and snow-clad mountains. Toby and Andrew wanted nothing more than to leap off the boat and hike to the summits. I've now grown used to the Canyon, but at first I felt somewhat nervous. Everything was so big, so high, so wild — and scarcely a soul in sight, except for a few miners panning for gold along the river and handfuls of people waiting at the landings — which were few and far between.

When the stern-wheeler stopped at a landing in the middle of nowhere — with only a couple of buildings — my heart dropped and I asked Mama, "Is *that* Yale?" She did not know. But then a passenger — Mr. Bailey, who works at the Hudson Bay Store — told us that Yale was another mile and a half up the river and we were stopping at the Powder Magazine to unload explosives.

Mama was clearly horrified. I remember her saying, "We have been travelling on a steamer packed with EXPLOSIVES?"

The man merely shrugged and said that A.O. — that is what everyone calls Andrew Onderdonk — needed explosives to blast out tunnels for his railway and this was the only way he could get them here.

A short time later we came in sight of Yale. Great Godfrey! The town swarmed like an anthill with throngs of people — all of them here to build the railway — and freight wagons moving back and forth.

And buildings! There were five hotels on Front Street alone! And all new because of a recent fire. Mr. Bailey said that Yale was an "up-and-coming town with a prosperous future" — or something like that. Mama said it looked like a rough town without a trace of Gentility.

This was true! For when we got off the steamboat a group of children ran out from behind a building and threw pine cones at my brothers and me and shouted, "Smarty boots, proudy hoops!" I later discovered that Rachel Perkins was amongst them and so were Rusty Schroeder and his sister Clara, and his friend Finch, but at the time I saw them as a bunch of horrid little ruffians and I wanted to return to Ottawa that very minute. But then I spotted Papa. I was so happy to see him I forgot about Ottawa and ruffians and everything else in the world.

Papa gave us a quick tour of Yale on the way to our house. There were two streets running parallel with the river, and a few cross streets. Now, as I look out my window, I see it is pretty much the same. On Front Street there is the Railway office, the Express and Stage Line, hotels and saloons and warehouses and stores — like Schroeder's Butcher Shop (Rusty's father's) and the Chemist Shop that is presently waiting for a new owner. Behind Front Street there is Douglas Street and our church, St. John the Divine, that was built for the miners during the Gold Rush over twenty years ago.

The day we arrived, Papa pointed out everything and gave long explanations. First, in the east end of town — Chinatown, the Indian community, railway shops under construction, the great Cariboo Wagon Road that was built by the Royal Engineers so that supplies could get up to the gold-mining towns and so on and so forth. Mercy McGinnis! I was too overwhelmed to take it *all* in — except for Clair's

Bakery and Confectionery where we stopped for lemon sticks.

After that we went to the west end of town. It is very pretty, with houses and flower gardens and orchards. And at last we circled back and came to our new house — up behind Douglas Street and close to the Accident Hospital and St. John's.

We had a grand time exploring our house. I still remember Mama's excitement when she discovered the brand new, *huge* black cooking range in the kitchen. You would think she had discovered a gold mine. What I liked the best — and still do — is the cottonwood tree that grows outside my bedroom window, especially in the spring when the buds smell like honey.

Our house is bigger than the one we left in Ottawa, but not as big as Mr. Onderdonk's. He has a grand house west of here, not far from the Powder Works Factory. He comes from New York and I suppose he deserves a mansion, since he is in charge of building the entire Pacific Section of the railway. Papa says that A.O. is very clever and a top-notch organizer. Everything he needs for the railway, he builds himself. He needs rolling stock and special cars to transport building materials and to carry out inspections, so he sets up a Machine Shop and Car Shop to build them. Since we came to Yale, he has built a Powder Works Factory to make explosives, so he no longer has to bring them on the steamer. He has also built a Turn Table and Round House with three stalls for Locomotive Engines. He does not do all this himself, of course. He has drillers and carpenters, machinists and blacksmiths, and men of all trades. And he does not build the locomotives, he buys them from the United States.

Papa often says he is proud to be a Bridge Foreman working for a contractor like A.O. Well, I hope A.O. is proud to have my Papa working for him.

Now my fingers are cramped from writing so much about nothing — except Past History.

Later

I've been following my Pledge to the letter, especially since Princess Louise will soon be here. It amuses my brothers to see me gliding from room to room with a book on my head. Toby dares me to use Mama's massive *Pilgrim's Progress* rather than my thin volume of poetry but I steadfastly refuse. *Pilgrim's Progress* weighs more than I do. And I can't be gracious with a broken neck.

I often catch Mama shaking her head as if to say, What is happening to our Kate?

I admit this ladylike behaviour is an enormous strain.

Mercy Mackerel! The lamp is smoking dreadfully. I'd best blow it out before I go blind.

LESSON LEARNED: Clean the chimney and replace the wick so Mama will not have to remind me again.

Now it is 10 oClock and time for bed.

Sunday, September 17

Took a walk upriver with Mama. Saw Indians at every bend catching salmon in dip nets and drying them in the sun. They were drying huckleberries, too.

Mama stopped to admire an enormous, freshly caught salmon. "That's twenty-five pounds if it's an ounce," she said — and the next thing I knew, the Indians had sold her the whole thing for a penny a pound. Mama was pleased, considering the price of mutton is fifteen cents a pound.

At first I thought we would have to carry the salmon home. But the Indians said they'd clean it and deliver it to our door. And they did. So now we have a huge headless salmon stinking up the house.

Toby informed us that since Papa is back at camp, the four of us would have to eat about six pounds each before it spoiled. Mama told him to stop talking and get it into the ice box.

Boiled salmon and dressed cucumbers for supper.

Monday, September 18

I have a new friend and her name is Anne Swanson. She is very pale and thin — but pretty — with blue eyes and hair so fair it looks white. She suffers from *anemia,* which means poverty of the blood. Her father is the new owner of the Chemist Shop.

Anne comes from Winnipeg and she is in the Fourth Reader like me. Now our school has sixteen girls and twenty-six boys.

Today at lunch I saw Rusty and Finch take Anne's lunch pail and run off to the boys' outhouse. It made me so cross I threw all my hard-earned Social Graces out the window and ran straight in after them — much to everyone's horror — and yelled, "Give me that, you great big bullies!" And I snatched Anne's lunch pail before they had a chance to dump its contents down the hole. Poor little Oliver Kustner was squirming by the other hole, desperate for me to get out. He need not have worried, as I did *not* want to linger.

Anne was crying in the corner of the schoolyard and I gave her her lunch pail. Then I got my own lunch and we ate together under the willows. I tried to cheer her up — told her she is *very lucky* she has a school to go to. I arrived in Yale in late September, 1880, after the old school burnt down. It was ten months before they started to build a new one, and all that time we had no proper classes. Papa said if ignorance were bliss, the children in Yale must be the happiest in the country. Anne couldn't help but smile when I told her that.

I also told her that Mama made sure we kept up with our lessons, in spite of our grumbling. She even made us read *Pilgrim's Progress*. But the worst thing about having no school was that I never had a chance to make friends. The only time I saw other girls was at Church or in town, and they were all too old or too young to be *Best* Friends. Except for Rachel who was too mean, but only at first. I used to cry buckets, I was that homesick for our house in Ottawa and my Best Friend, Mary Beth.

Then when the new school was ready and I thought, Hurray!, there was an outbreak of scarlet fever and all the children in town were kept at home. Mama would not even let us go outside our gate. But finally, last October, we got to go to school.

Anne said, "I bet the boys weren't mean to *you*."

HA! I told her about my first week, when two big boys — who later moved away from Yale, thank goodness — kept throwing my lunch down the hole. They said if I told, they would throw me down, too. Well, my brothers found out and threw away *their* lunches instead. That cheered Anne up! Then Teacher rang the bell and we went inside.

After school, Anne asked if I had a Best Friend. I

told her all about Rachel and she asked if I would be *her* Best Friend, as long as Rachel was in Spuzzum. I said I would be pleased as punch. And I am! Anne is nine months younger than me but she is the only girl in school who is closest to my age and in the same Reader.

Anne is very lucky, she has two little sisters, Charlotte and Rose. I wish my sisters were still alive. Marian would be eleven years old and Laura would be ten. If they had not died, I'd never have to worry about moving to a new place and making new friends. I'd never be lonely. I'd be like Toby and Andrew, who always have each other.

My sisters died a long time ago, of scarlet fever, only 2 weeks apart. I was too little to remember — only that Mama cried and cried and hugged me so hard it hurt.

I'm happy to have Anne for a friend. I also feel a bit anxious — because what if she moves away like Rachel? Or what if *we* have to move again? Mama says, "Don't count your chickens before they hatch." But sometimes I just can't help it. Now I am all the more determined to be ladylike so I won't be banished to Angela College.

For supper tonight we had boiled salmon with curry sauce.

Tuesday, September 19

Blasting! My head aches.

Toby said he wants to quit school and work for the railway. He says it would be thrilling to climb the cliffs and dangle from ropes and set explosives. I said, "When they take you into the Hospital we can see *your* brains."

Andrew said, "No fear of that."

Later

A smelly chore today. I helped Mama prepare collared salmon by rolling up pieces of fish (once she'd removed the bones), tying them firmly and laying them in the kettle. Then we covered them with vinegar and boiling water and let them simmer.

For supper we naturally had collared salmon. Andrew told us that salmon is "brain food" and offered Toby his remaining 5½-pound share.

Poor Toby. He is one year older than me but only in the Third Reader.

Wednesday, September 20

Salmon cutlets for supper. Mama says we're looking smarter already.

Thursday, September 21

Princess Louise will be here in 10 days! She is presently in Victoria with her husband, the Governor General, but after Victoria they are going across the Strait to New Westminster, then up the Fraser River to Emory and then on to Yale by train. I wonder what Princess Louise will think of our Canyon.

Teacher says Princess Louise is the first member of the Royal Family to visit this part of the Empire, so it is a Very Great Occasion.

Anne and I are determined to think of something special to give the Princess. But Great Godfrey, she must have *everything*.

After school today I went to the *Sentinel* and Mr. Hagan let me "play the devil" — which means I acted as his apprentice! I smeared the face of the type with greasy black printer's ink, then shoved the roller back and forth across the type. Then I helped him fold and address the papers. I offered to help deliver them to his customers, but he said he liked to distribute the goods himself. Except for our copy, which he let me bring home.

In the excitement of the day I completely forgot my Pledge to act ladylike. I ran like a wild thing and failed to hide my exuberance. And when Mama saw my ink-stained hands, horrors! Out came the lemon juice. Scrub, scrub, scrub until the skin was peeling. No grumbling, though. Not when I am about to meet a Princess.

Friday, September 22

I wish Papa were a gold miner like Mr. Stout across the river. He is giving his little girls, Margaret and Mary, some gold specimens and they are going to present one to His Excellency the Governor General and the other to Princess Louise. The card will say "from the youngest miners in British Columbia."

Anne and I cannot think of a present. Andrew says he'll shoot us a grouse and we can give the feathers. Anne found this very funny but Andrew wasn't joking. His room is full of feathers. Not merely from the game he shoots, but feathers he finds in the woods. Some of them are very pretty. But not worthy of a Princess.

Papa came home in time for supper. He ate three large helpings of potted salmon — hurray! fewer pounds left for us! — and two helpings of apple pie. Then he lit his pipe and leaned back to tell us the railway news. He says the progress is *very* slow because there is so much tunnelling and rock cutting and blasting to be done, and the Wagon Road is in such a terrible state the supplies cannot get through, and there is always the unexpected, like yesterday, when tons of rock fell on the track near Sailor's Bluff and had to be cleared.

I soon got bored with railway problems and Wagon Road problems but I remembered my Social Graces and pretended to be interested by saying nothing, nodding as if in agreement and smiling often. I also sat up straight and tall without a book on my head. No Angela College for me! I was already the height of Refinement and Grace.

I thought I was succeeding admirably. Until Andrew said my head would roll off if I didn't stop bobbing it and Toby told me to stop pulling faces. Papa stopped talking railway and asked if I was feeling all right.

Mercy Mackerel! I wanted to say, "Here I am, turning over a new leaf so you won't banish me to Victoria, and no one even notices!" Instead, I pleaded a headache and asked to be excused.

I'm growing weary of the struggle to be "Lady Kate." Is this what Princess Louise has to go through? Or does a Princess naturally act like a Princess without any effort?

The good news about today is that Papa said he would take me to Spuzzum next month to see Rachel. I hope the road is in good repair by then. I can be the real Kate with Rachel. She is every bit as wild as I am — even more so, in Mama's opinion.

Almost forgot — the *Skuzzy* has finally made it

through Hell's Gate. Mr. Onderdonk decided to *pull* the steamboat through the rapids. He got 150 Chinese workers to line up on both sides of the river and pull on ropes that were attached to the boat. Now the railway is happy because the *Skuzzy* will carry supplies between Boston Bar and Lytton. And I am happy because I will not have to listen to any more talk about the *Skuzzy*.

Saturday, September 23

Spent the morning helping Mama preserve more collared salmon. But this time we put it in wide-mouthed jars and added more vinegar to preserve it. So we will not have to eat it all at once. Mama says we'll appreciate the taste come January. I think not.

Went to Yale Creek with Toby and Andrew and caught six trout. *Nothing* tastes as good as fresh trout, certainly not collared or potted or boiled salmon. Andrew suggested we give Princess Louise a trout. When I told him he had no respect, he said, "Don't fret, Louise, I'd gut it first." At least *he* calls me Louise.

On the way home I had an idea so I went straight to Anne's house and said, "Let's give the Princess some jade!"

At first she gave me a blank look, but when I told her that jade is a precious stone and it is found in the

Fraser River, she said, "That is a splendid idea!" So tomorrow afternoon, if we are allowed, we are going to look for jade.

Anne wasn't the least bit eager when I said we could cast for trout at the same time. Fishing? Horrors! She cannot believe I bait my own hooks and gaff the fish when I reel them in. She says there will be snow in July before she does such gruesome things. It is obvious she does not have brothers. Or maybe it is the anemia that makes her squeamish.

Sunday, September 24

Church this morning. All through Rev. Horlock's sermon we heard explosions — and railway cars clang-clanging through town as loudly as usual. Mama says it is a disgrace that Sunday is no longer a day of rest. At least we have a rest from school.

Mama wanted me to stay home this afternoon and "behave like Sunday," but I pleaded with her to let me find some jade for the Princess — she'll be here in just over a week. I promised Mama I would think Sunday thoughts the whole way and sing hymns when I got home and read extra passages from the Bible, so she finally said I could go.

Anne had a time convincing her mother *and* her father — he doesn't work on Sundays, not like Papa — but they eventually relented and we set off after lunch.

The Wagon Road was so busy we nearly got run over — first by the Express, then by a ten-yoke ox team hauling freight, then by two pack trains of mules.

We reached the jade spot and I was about to start down the bank when Anne grabbed my arm and said, "We can't go down there! There's a camp with Chinamen!"

I was astonished, not only by her words but by the look of horror on her face. I could not imagine why *that* would upset her. When I told her they were there all the time, just two men mining jade and minding their own business, she fair near hit the roof. "You *knew*? And you failed to tell me?" She said she never would have come had she known. Her mother would not have allowed it. She'd heard that hundreds of Chinese had died of smallpox and we would catch it for sure. Or else we would be murdered the minute our backs were turned.

I told her that some Chinese had died of scurvy, not smallpox, but that only got her wailing about how we would catch scurvy.

Great Godfrey! I reckoned the day would be over before we went down the river bank, let alone found any jade. I told her what Mama told me: you do not get scurvy if you eat fruits and vegetables and fresh meat. The Chinese workers got scurvy because they only ate rice and dried salmon. As for being murdered? Poppycock!

I might as well have been talking to a catfish for all the good it did. She wanted to forget the jade and go home. I finally persuaded her otherwise, after promising we would go a fair distance away from the camp.

As we started down the bank, she said, "Chinaman, Chinaman, never die. Yellow face and slanty eye."

Good thing Papa wasn't there. We were in Kwong Lee's store one day and he heard me chant that same rhyme. Quick as a whistle he marched me home and tanned my backside. I cried buckets and told him it wasn't fair, I heard people talk like that all the time, even grown-ups. He said that did not make it right — the Chinese were good men and hard workers and I was never to talk about people in a cruel or mocking way, no matter what their race.

I did not tell Anne all that, but I should have. The whole time I was looking for jade she kept watch to make sure we were not being followed. To make matters worse, when I finally found a piece of jade she turned up her nose and said, "It doesn't look precious. It looks like an ordinary rock."

Well, of course it looks like a rock. It *is* a rock! Anyone knows that. It has to be cut and polished to look precious. But no use telling Anne.

On the way home I picked a bouquet of flowers — purple Michaelmas daisies, white everlasting and yellow goldenrod. I'm going to dry the flowers and arrange them in a little glass dome — like they sell at the General Store — and give it to Mama for Christmas.

We passed a gang of Chinese and Anne once again said her rhyme — but this time very quietly. I told her if she was worried about the Chinese, she should have been here when I first came to Yale. On pay days, Mama would not let us outside our gates — not even Andrew and Toby — because of all the fighting and drunken *white* men stumbling about.

Anne shrugged and after that we scarcely spoke at all. It was a long walk home and I am sorry to say I did not think Sunday thoughts — I thought about how much fun it would have been if Rachel could have come instead of Anne.

I also thought about the Chinese workers. I still remember when the first lot arrived in Yale. We came out of church and saw the flatcars passing through town, loaded with hundreds and hundreds of Chinese. My brothers and I stood there gawking until Mama told us we'd be swallowing flies if we didn't close our mouths. We were accustomed to the Chinese because of the ones who had stayed in Yale after the Gold Rush, but we had never seen so many all at once. And then Papa told us that Mr. Onderdonk was bringing in more — maybe 5000 or more! — because the white workers he'd hired from San Francisco were hopeless. Some had shown up at the railway camps dressed in tattered suits and most couldn't tell one end of a shovel from the other.

I have never seen any Chinese workers drunk, not like some of those Whites. But now the gangs are too far up the line to come into Yale very often. When they do, they mostly behave. Mama says Yale has turned into a respectable little town. So now we are allowed out of the gates — and even up the Wagon Road.

Thank goodness I have my Diary. It is like talking to a friend who is interested in *everything* I have to say. Not like Anne. I wish I hadn't rescued her lunch from the outhouse.

LESSON LEARNED: Next time I look for jade I'll ask my brothers to come with me.

Monday, September 25

Horrid day at school. Teacher yelled at me for daydreaming — I could not help it, I'm too excited about the Princess — and Anne would not speak to me. But I heard her tell her sister not to pull faces at the Chinese passing in front of the school. So maybe she took some of my words to heart.

Wednesday, September 27

Another railway worker went into the Accident Hospital today. He was about to blast a stump when the charge accidentally exploded. I pray that Papa never gets hurt.

Saturday, September 30

Tomorrow night Princess Louise will arrive in Yale. On Monday the Governor General will give an address and we will have a holiday from school in order to hear it. Then the G-G and the Princess are going on flatcars up the line.

Everyone is excited. The streets are being cleaned and an arch has been put up on Front Street. It is thirty feet high. There is a Union Jack at each of the four corners of the arch and a higher one in the centre with the Royal Scottish Standard. And fancy lettering that says *Welcome Lorne and Louise.*

Anne and I are friends again. She came to my house and we wrapped our jade. We did not have time to cut it or polish it, but I think one of the Princess's servants can do that. She likely has hundreds of them.

On the card I wrote *To Princess Louise from Miss Louise Cameron and Miss Anne Swanson.* I told Anne her name could go first but she said my name should go first since it was my idea and I found the jade.

We cut out large red letters saying *Welcome Louise* and pasted them to white paper. Then we made a wreath of evergreens and flowers to go around it. Everyone in town got little flags to wave and we put ours in the wreath. Anne's father said our wreath was so grand we could hang it from their balcony. They live close to the arch so the Princess will have a perfect view of it. And we will have a perfect view of *her* because up on the balcony is where we are going to be!

The town looks like a fairyland. There are decorations all along the railway track, and every store has wreaths, flowers, evergreens and flags. Even the saloons and the Chinese stores. There are fir trees placed all along the procession route, and Union Jacks waving as far as the eye can see, and the Hudson Bay Company flag, too. Everyone's verandah has hanging baskets with hundreds of flowers. Mama's baskets look spectacular.

At Schroeder's Butcher Shop there is a display of evergreens arranged around a carcass of mutton. Toby saw it and said we should add a few trout.

Monday, October 2

Hell's Gate and Galoshes! I am crushed beyond words.

Waited all morning for the Princess to arrive. At

11:00 we heard the whistle of the engine coming up from Emory and people started running to the railway platform at Victoria Street. I wanted to go, too, but I remembered my Pledge and refrained. So we waited some more and practised our curtseys (easy) and patience (difficult). The balcony was crowded — Anne, her parents and sisters and Mama and me and a few neighbours. My brothers were at the platform.

Finally we heard the cheers and knew the cars had arrived. We saw Mr. Fraser — in Highland dress — marching and playing his bagpipes. Then the dapple greys came into view, pulling the coach. We had bouquets at the ready but then we saw that Princess Louise wasn't there! Nobody else seemed to mind. They cheered and threw their bouquets. One struck the G-G on his shoulder and he looked up and smiled — directly at Anne.

I did not throw my bouquet. I wanted to throw a trout. I wanted to go home but Mama said I had to stay for the speeches.

Bullocks and Boredom, the speeches. Rev. Horlock gave his speech and said everyone was sorry the Princess could not come. Then the G-G gave his speech and said she would have come if *he* had not thought the journey up country would be too tiring.

Mercy McGinnis! Does Princess Louise not have

a mind of her own? She could have come as far as Yale and rested here.

Anne kept nudging me and said we should go down and give him our present. But I decided right then and there I would *not* give away the jade. I told Anne I had changed my mind. Mama told me to stop scowling.

After the speeches, Margaret and Mary Stout gave the G-G their gold specimens and the procession carried on through the town.

Now Anne is mad at me for being pig-headed. Mama is mad at me for being peevish. And I'm back to being Kate. Naturally, now that I no longer like it, Toby calls me Louise.

Peevish: perversely obstinate and ill-tempered.

Tuesday, October 3

Sunny.

Teacher quizzed us about the G-G's visit to make sure we had not taken the day off to go trout fishing. Then we had to write out the G-G's full name and titles for penmanship: *His Excellency the Right Honourable Sir John Douglas Sutherland Campbell, Marquis of Lorne, Knight of the Most Ancient and Most Noble Order of the Thistle, Knight Grand Cross of the Most Distinguished Order of St. Michael and St. George, Governor General of Canada.* He must have the longest name and title in the world. But long name or not, he should have let the Princess come to Yale.

Anne is still mad. I overheard her telling Clara about the jade and they both said I was stubborn and mean — especially since the jade was meant to be a present from Anne as well as from me. They said the Princess would have been pleased as punch to have something from Yale when she could not be here in person. They said I was selfish and always had to have my own way. I pretended I didn't hear them.

What does a Knight of the Thistle do? I asked Andrew on the way home from school and he said that was a *prickly* question!

I said we should form our own Noble Order of Knights but call it something different. We had lots of ideas — Most Noble Order of the Dogwood. Or Huckleberry. Toby liked Most Noble Order of the Trout. We could not reach an agreement so for now we will be like the G-G and call ourselves Knights of the Thistle.

Mama sent me to Schroeder's for mutton chops — just as a big flock of sheep was coming through Yale. I had to wait ages to cross the street. Someone said there were 500.

Now it is bedtime. If I can't get to sleep I know what sheep to count. They are all on their way to Victoria.

Rain and mud.

School seemed empty today because a lot of pupils are sick with whooping cough, including Anne and Clara. Teacher had fewer pupils to torment so he picked on me. He asked the most taxing questions in Mental Arithmetic and I disgraced myself by not knowing the answers. If it takes 20 yards of calico to make 2 dresses, how many similar dresses will 110 yards make? And: What is the value of a load of oats weighing 1037 lbs. at 40¢ a bushel?

Bushels, bullocks, bother! Naturally I know the answers now, when Teacher is not standing over me looking cross. He gave me the entire book of Mental Arithmetic so I can practise before the Examination — which is over two months away, so what is the point?

I suppose I should get at it instead of renting my spleen by copying the bothersome questions into my Diary.

What is a spleen?

Saw another accident victim go into the Hospital as we were coming home from school. It was Papa's friend, Mr. Ferguson. He thought all the shots had exploded, so he went back into the tunnel and one of the shots went off. He was hit in the back of the head by a rock.

Thursday, October 5, Early Morning

Terrible night. First I had the nightmare, the one about Papa being hurt. I woke up crying and could not get back to sleep so Mama came in and told me not to worry, that Papa is in God's hands and our prayers will keep him safe.

But aren't the other workers in God's hands, too? Why do *they* get hurt? I asked Mama but she didn't know the answer. She only said, "God works in mysterious ways."

I said some more prayers and finally went back to sleep but then the wind woke me up. Mercy Mackerel! It felt as if the four winds of Heaven were blowing through our house.

Walked to school in the wind and rain and mud.

More pupils are away with whooping cough — over half the school — so now I am the oldest girl. And because I am the oldest girl, Teacher let me help some Primaries with their reading — Melissa Fox, Hughie McDonald and Oliver Kustner. We did a poem in the Second Primer called "Be a Man." Here's the first verse.

Do not cry. If you hit your toe,
Say, "Oh!" And let it go.
Be a man if you can,
And do not cry.

It is not much of a poem. My favourite line — which I recited to my brothers — is in the second verse: *Do not tease your little sister.* Melissa liked that one, too. She has three brothers but she is not the little sister, she is the Big Sister. Even though she is only seven.

Hughie and Oliver had only recently begun the Second Primer and were more interested in looking at the pictures than in reading.

It is the first time Teacher has allowed me to help the little ones and I enjoyed it immensely. I think Melissa and the boys enjoyed it, too — especially Melissa. I had them read the poem again and again until they could enunciate every syllable clearly. Then Hughie took on such a spell of coughing we had to stop. Later I learned he was faking the cough, the cheeky rascal.

After school, Teacher told me I was a big help! I asked if I could do it again and he smiled and raised his right eyebrow. Does that mean *yes*? Does the left eyebrow mean *no*? I will have to figure it out.

Friday, October 6

This morning on the way to school I used the expression "rent my spleen" and Andrew told me I had it wrong. It is "vent my spleen," and it has to do with bad temper.

A spleen, according to Andrew, is an organ near the stomach. I find it a most unappetizing word so I do not care to use it — or vent it — again.

Teacher's right eyebrow must mean *yes* because I helped the little ones again today! I hope the older girls stay away for a long time. Anne, too. At least Papa's taking me to Spuzzum in a fortnight to see Rachel. Otherwise I am doomed to being friendless.

Came home straight after school. Laid the cloth for supper. Set the table. Ate supper. Swept up the crumbs in the dining room. Helped Mama wash the dishes. Put away the supper things and swept the kitchen. And Andrew complains of *his* chores. I offered to chop firewood or rake out the ashes if he would bake bread or black-lead the range. The look on his face, you would think he had eaten a bucket of milk porridge.

Saturday, October 7

I'm in bed and dying of whooping cough.

So is Toby. Andrew is spared — I do not know why.

Papa said he'll take me to Rachel's next month instead of this month, now that I'm sick. But the road will be worse and I will most likely be dead. Poor me.

Thursday, October 19

The worst is over. After 2 weeks of wracking coughs and burning mustard plastered to my chest, I am slowly coming back to life — although I'm still forced to take Syrup of Squill's every 4 hours to ease my cough. SQUILL'S! The name itself is enough to make me vomit. Mama says I should not complain because when she was a little girl and had whooping cough, the doctor treated her with leeches.

Mr. Hagan brought over a bag of horehound candy. The licorice taste is a treat.

Friday, October 20

More rain.

Our neighbour, Mr. Harrison, stopped by for a visit and stayed for tea. He told Mama he thinks that Yale should have a Library and a Reading Room. He is asking anyone with used books or magazines to donate them so we can get started. He wants to raise money to purchase new books, too. I asked him if children could use the library and he said certainly, provided their parents pay the required fee.

I think this is a grand idea so I'm going to donate some of the magazines that Grandma Forrest sends from England. We've got lots — like the *Girl's Own Paper* and *Boy's Own Paper* and more coming all the time. I can't wait to use the library.

Saturday, October 21

The Skuzzy Creek bridge is almost finished. So far everyone working on it has been safe, including Papa.

Monday, October 23

Hip, hip, hurray! I went back to school today and Melissa was so happy to see me, she asked Teacher if I could help her with her Reading again. He raised his right eyebrow and said Yes! — provided I finish my own work first.

Anne was back, too. She said she had heard I was sick and she hoped I was feeling better. We got scolded for talking and giggling and hip, hip, hurraying, but Teacher took pity for once and did not rap our knuckles or make us write lines. He just raised his *left* eyebrow — a warning signal! — and gave us a fearsome scowl.

Anne must have recovered from the jade fiasco as well as from the whooping cough because she did not mention it once. Neither did I. Thank goodness we are friends again.

Tuesday, October 24

Rain and mud. Nothing ever happens in my dreary life. I can't even raise one eyebrow at a time.

Wednesday, October 25

Last spring Papa said that by fall, the whistle of the "Iron Horse" would be heard throughout the Canyon. And he was right. I love the sound. One day it will echo across the whole Dominion of Canada. And the rails will stretch across the land like a ribbon of shining steel.

Thursday, October 26

I loved doing Penmanship today:
Round the rugged rock the rapid river ran.
It sounds like the Fraser!

Friday, October 27

Mr. Hagan printed a poem in the *Sentinel*. I asked him if he is the author but he refused to say. It is called "The Song of the Locomotive" and is very stirring. It has ten verses. These are my favourites:

Beware! Beware! for I come in my might!
With a scream, and a scowl of scorn;
With a speed like the mountain eagle's flight
When he rides the breeze of morn!

Away — away — o'er valley and plain,
I sweep with a voice of wrath —

In a fleecy cloud I wrap my train
As I tread my iron path!

My bowels are fire and my arm is steel,
My breath is a rolling cloud –
And my voice peals out as I onward wheel,
Like the thunder rolling loud!

I roar on the beach of the roaring deep
When the sea-shells touch my wheels –
Through the desert land with a howl I sweep
And the yellow harvest fields.

I traverse the regions of burning heat –
The Equator hears my scream –
And I breathe the silence of winter's retreat,
Where the glittering snow-fields gleam.

The wild beasts fly when my voice they hear,
Through the sounding forest ring,
And the sons of men stand mute with fear,
Of Earth I am King!

I love this poem. I'm going to learn it by heart and recite it whenever I walk along the tracks or when I take the train across Canada — or even when I visit the Equator!

I wonder what it is like on the Equator, besides hot. I wonder if Mr. Hagan composed the poem and is simply being modest. I would not be modest if I had written such a splendid poem.

Saturday, October 28

More rain. More mud.

Caught Toby pouring cod liver oil down the sink. He planned to fill the bottle with tea — the same colour as cod liver oil — and asked if I would help. He did not need to ask twice. Swallowing rotten fish in liquid form is truly a disgusting form of torture and we Knights of the Thistle must resist. When the tea was ready we poured it into the bottle and put the bottle back in the cupboard.

Andrew came home a while later, drenched to the skin, but with a fine buck. Now we can look forward to roast venison with Mama's Old English Jelly Wine Sauce that makes everything taste better.

We told Andrew about the cod liver oil and swore him to Secrecy.

Sunday, October 29

Dismal, dreary, rainy day.

Mama opened the bottle of "cod liver oil" and knew it was tea. Hell's Gate and Galoshes! — have I not suffered enough with the whooping cough?

Wednesday, November 1

Anne's birthday is coming up — it's on Saturday, November 11, and today she handed out invitations to her party. I told her I can't go because I'm going to Spuzzum to see Rachel and not even an earthquake will keep me away this time.

Anne looked a little disappointed and asked if I couldn't go to Rachel's another time. No! I said. Even if I could, I wouldn't want to. We're going to ride horses and have all sorts of Adventures!

Thursday, November 2

Snow in the mountains! Soon we can go sledding.

Saturday, November 4

Dull, dreary day and a mood to match. I asked Anne if she wanted to go for a stroll but she said she was busy. So I walked up the river by myself and looked for jade. I came home empty-handed without having a shadow of an Adventure.

Monday, November 6

Today at school Anne asked me why I always walked as if I had a yardstick taped to my back. She said it looked very odd and made everyone laugh.

To prove her point, she told me to turn around. And when I did I saw Clara and the other girls — except Melissa — giggling and pointing at me.

I'm hurt to the bone. How could Anne make such a cruel remark? Surely she is not still fretting about the jade. That happened over a month ago! How could anyone hold a grudge for that long?

Thank goodness I'm going to Rachel's on Saturday. I wish I could stay in Spuzzum forever.

Friday, November 10

Papa came home with dreadful news. A huge blast went off and a piece of rock was thrown so far it hit a Chinese worker and *cut off his head*.

Papa said the Chinese gang blamed the foreman because he had not given proper warning. No wonder they were angry. They chased the foreman into the river up to his neck and threw stones from the bank. Someone finally appeared in a boat and rescued him. And then the Chinese fired shots and two bullets hit the water close to the boat.

Now it is bedtime and I should get to sleep. Tomorrow I'll see Rachel! But tonight, I hope I don't have nightmares. Papa is a Bridge Foreman — what if something goes wrong and all his workers chase him into the river and throw stones?

Saturday, November 11

Aspen Hill Farm, Spuzzum

It is very late. Rachel and I are curled up in her bed, wide awake with talk and giggles and plans and Excitement. Mrs. Perkins has just come in and told us to be quiet and get to sleep. But we can't sleep. So Rachel has lit a lamp and we are presently engaged in recording the events of the day in our Diaries.

I left Yale early this morning with Papa on the Express coach for Spuzzum. Mr. Tingley was driving a six-horse team and the leaders were so spirited and anxious they reared up and almost got tangled in the harness. After the first 100 yards or so they settled down to a brisk trot and nothing distracted them.

It was a thrilling ride but also very frightening. In some places the railway track is high up the bank and the Wagon Road is beside the river. A slide could come down at any time because of all the rain and mud. And the bluffs! The road goes around on struts that overhang the Fraser River hundreds of feet below. There is a rule that says the lighter traffic, like the Express, takes the outside of the road and the heavy traffic, like ox teams with six, eight or ten yoke of oxen, have to take the inside. The road is only 18 feet wide. So every time we passed an ox team we were off to the outside edge clinging for dear life.

A fine shaking we had in that coach, scrunching over stones and into potholes as deep as a ditch. Papa said that when the railway is finished we'll feel like we're riding on silk.

We saw lots of deer on the road, and a coyote, but no bears because of the season, and no panthers. Once before, on another trip, I saw a panther cross the road in front of us.

All along the way we saw railway workers — gangs of track layers carrying heavy wooden ties on their shoulders (two men to a tie) and placing them on the roadbed, gangs laying down the steel rails and bolting them together, gangs hammering in the iron spikes to hold the rails in place. Then another gang spreads gravel and sand between the ties so the track is steady. And after all that, the foreman comes along and lies down on the rail and looks with one eye to make sure the track is even.

We passed bunkhouse camps where the white workers live, tent camps where the Chinese live, and hundreds of Chinese workers. They are in gangs, too, about thirty in a gang and every Chinese gang has a white boss. They were drilling and blasting and removing the rock to get the roadbed ready for the gangs who followed.

I'm writing this down before I forget because

Papa says it is important. So when the Railway is finished and I'm riding across Canada on the train I'll remember not only the famous men like Andrew Onderdonk and our Prime Minister, Sir John A. Macdonald — and of course, the Very Famous John Stuart Cameron (Papa's joke!) — but all the *ordinary* workers who made it possible.

Today was fairly mild for November, but all along the line we saw fires and huge teapots so the Chinese could warm themselves and drink their tea. Papa said they feel the cold most sorely, since the part of China they come from is very warm.

A passenger in the coach said, "Pity they didn't stay there."

Papa's mouth turned into a thin line, the way it does when he is angry. But he held his tongue.

On the way we passed some of Papa's bridges. He calls them "grasshopper trestles." They do look like grasshoppers, with long post-legs on the outside standing in steps cut into the rock, and short post-legs on the other side because there's only half a roadbed. Papa said they have to build the bridges that way to get around some of the bluffs.

We got to Spuzzum — 12 miles above Yale — and there was Rachel, waiting to give me a hug. I kissed Papa goodbye — he has to go up-country to Lytton — and got into the wagon with Rachel and her brother, Adam. For fun, Adam took us across the

Alexandra Suspension Bridge a mile above Spuzzum. The river there is tremendously swift and deep — to think that Rachel and I ventured upon it in a very small boat.

Adam stopped the horse in the middle of the Bridge so we could admire the view — mossy rocks, fir trees, boiling river — but the poor horse was not impressed. He was skittery and impatient to be back on solid ground.

Rachel and I chattered like chipmunks all the way to Aspen Hill Farm. We laughed about how much we had hated each other when I first came to Yale. She said I put on Big City Airs the way I tippy-toed down the street — I did not! — and I said she was as mean as a rusty nail and a ruffian besides. That is how it was until we ended up at the same fishing spot with our brothers and Rachel fell into the creek — showing off — and I went to her rescue and we became Best Friends.

All this time, Adam hadn't said Boo, but then he said I should have left Rachel in the creek! He warned us we had better not be planning to run the rapids this time — at least, not in *his* boat. We gave him our Solemn Word.

When we got to the Farm I gave Mrs. Perkins the six jars of preserved salmon Mama had sent up, and told little Becky how much she's grown. They both seemed very pleased.

We had roast chicken for lunch. I was enjoying it immensely, until Becky told me it was Harold, her pet rooster. That explained why she only ate mashed potatoes. Poor Becky. I have to admit Harold was tasty.

After lunch Rachel and I helped with the washing-up and then we went riding. She rode her horse, Fireweed, and I rode Starlight. We galloped across the field as fast as the wind and came back along the Wagon Road.

We rubbed down the horses and Starlight nuzzled my cheek as if to say "thank you." I told Rachel she was so lucky, that I would give anything to live on a farm and have my own horse. At that, she burst into tears and told me she was going to Victoria in January and had to leave Fireweed behind. Why *Victoria*? Because her parents want her to have a proper education so they are sending her to Angela College.

Well! When I heard this my mood went from despair to exceedingly great joy. I told her that *my* parents were planning to send *me* to Angela College!

This cheered her up enormously. We danced around the barn, then kissed the horses and went inside.

We had cold mutton sandwiches for supper and Becky told me it was Radish, her pet sheep. Rachel's other brother, Simon — who had been off on some errands at lunch — said to pay her no mind as she is forever telling tales. Her only real pet is a cat. Which they are *not* planning to eat.

We played Charades after supper and then it was time for bed and here we are. Rachel is asleep. So I'm going to blow out the lamp and go to sleep, too. It was a wonderful day.

Sunday, November 12

Home again, after another eventful day.

This morning at Rachel's I was attacked by a rooster. I was collecting the eggs and when I reached under one of the hens, the way I do at home, she made such an almighty fuss the rooster flew to her defense — straight at my face. Rachel heard my screams, ran to my rescue and chased the rooster outside.

Mercy McGinnis! I could have lost an eye. If Rachel has to face that monster every morning, she is braver than I am. I told her she deserved to be in the Knights of the Thistle.

We had another gallop after breakfast, then lunch and then it was time to go.

I waited for the Express at Spuzzum, sad to say goodbye, but excited, too, because for the first time I was travelling on my own. But when I got on the Express, horrors! Rusty was there with his parents. I had no choice but to sit across from him — and he smiled, the cheek!

The coach was full, four passengers to a side, and every time we hit a rut in the road — every second, that is — we tumbled against each other and had a right good shake-up. The road was busy, even though it was Sunday — we went whipping around one curve and almost collided with a twelve-mule team.

Whenever I happened to look at Rusty — *not* on purpose but when I could not help it — he gave me the same little smile. He was quiet and polite, too, not loud and rude and silly like he is at school around Finch. And I noticed something odd. Whenever I caught his eye, my stomach went queasy. I'm certain it was because of the rough road. But there was a twinge of something I have never felt before.

Rusty's mother, Mrs. Schroeder, asked after Mama and her work at the Hospital, and Mr. Schroeder asked how Papa was doing and how the railway was progressing. I answered as best I could. Then they asked how Rusty was doing in school. Poor Rusty! His face turned as red as a beet. And I do not know why, but my stomach took another funny tumble.

Monday, November 13

Anne was very odd today. I told her about the splendid time I had with Rachel but she didn't seem interested, not even when I told her that we had eaten Becky's pets. She said maybe next time we would eat Rachel's horse. I laughed, thinking she was playing along with my joke, but then she said as serious as all get-out, "People do eat horses, you know, in places like France, for instance. Maybe what you thought was mutton was really a tough old horse." After that she linked arms with Clara and walked away.

I wonder when Mama is going to tell me about Angela College. I hope I can go with Rachel in January.

Wednesday, November 15

Andrew has taken up pyrography, where you burn a picture into a piece of wood. He is etching a design on a pipe rack to give Papa for Christmas. Naturally Toby is doing the same, only he is etching his design on a necktie holder. Now I know why their bedroom sometimes smells smoky — but only when Papa is away from home. They asked if I would like to try pyrography but I'm certain I would burn more fingers than wood.

I hope they're finished soon. I'm so afraid they might get careless and set the house on fire.

Hell's Gate and Gory Goblins! I could spit railway spikes. I will call upon Justice Crease himself and have that wicked Toby sentenced to death by hanging. Why? Because he found my Diary and took it to school and read parts of it *out loud* in the playground — my Private Thoughts about Anne being odd and how I wished I had not saved her lunch from the outhouse — and what I wrote about Rusty on the way back from Spuzzum. I could DIE with Humiliation. The rest of the day Anne refused to look at me, let alone talk to me. And Rusty — he smiled at me the whole livelong day.

I am presently in the chicken shed, sneezing every two minutes on account of the straw, and my eyes are stinging and red because of the torrents of tears I've shed these last few hours — and the hens are squawking and the rooster is giving me nasty looks as if he thinks I'm planning to move into his territory. I can hear Mama inside the house giving Toby an earful, with an abundance of "Wait til' your father gets home." GOOD! I will never forgive him.

He says he did it because I donated his *Boy's Own Paper*s to the library without asking his permission.

LESSON LEARNED.

I know it was wrong, I know I acted without thinking — but only because I was so excited by the prospect of a Lending Library. And I would have asked Toby if he had been home at the time, instead of gallivanting in the woods with Andrew. And if they had let me go with them, I would not have set myself the task of looking for magazines in the first place. But I apologized and got them back — all the *Boy's Own Papers* and the almanacs, too. I would have thought that was enough, but Toby was set on Revenge.

Thank goodness today is Friday. Perhaps by Monday Anne will have forgiven me, Rusty will have forgotten me, and the rest of the school will find someone else to torment. OHHH! Hateful horrid life. Hateful HORRID Toby.

Later

I'm back in my room after brushing off dust and straw and bits of grain. I smell of chickens and my head itches. All I need now is an attack of lice.

I may not be a reporter after all. Reporting an event or expressing an opinion that the WHOLE WORLD can read sounds exceedingly grand — but what if the World disagrees? Or takes it the wrong way, even if it is true? Mr. Hagan says you have to be thick-skinned and prepared to take it on the chin. I'm not sure if I can. I have a very small, thin-skinned chin.

Saturday, November 18

Mama made plum pudding today and now the whole house smells like Christmas — raisins and currants and candied peel, sugar and spices and brandy! Almonds, too! But no plums. Mama said in the olden days people made the pudding with dried plums — what we call prunes. Now they use currants and raisins instead.

We took turns stirring our Christmas wishes into the batter. Andrew reminded me to stir in the right direction. It has to be east to west because that is the direction the three Wise Men were travelling when they first saw the star in Bethlehem. He asked what I wished for but I refused to tell. Then I helped Mama stir in the silver charms. I hope I get the horseshoe this time. Last year I got the thimble and Toby called me Old Maid for weeks. I do not especially want a husband but I do NOT want to be an Old Maid. Are there any other choices?

Toby and I did not speak to each other all day.

Monday, November 20

Beastly day. Beastly school. My head still aches from being shouted at — not once but three times. Once for daydreaming, once for asking Teacher to repeat a question and a third time for failing to give the correct answer. Teacher got his "One hundred lines coming up" look and scowled his left eyebrow straight into his forehead. I thought I would die. But Toby whispered the correct answer and I was saved. Now I will have to forgive him for stealing my Diary.

Anne still won't speak to me. Is it because of the Diary or is she still holding a grudge from before? I tried to tell her that my Diary is full of nice things about her. But she walked away without listening. Clara told me I couldn't see the forest for the trees. What is that supposed to mean? Great Godfrey!

Thanks to Mama's plum-less pudding, our house still smells like Christmas. My one happy thought of the day.

Tuesday, November 21

Botany today. I drew a sketch of Shepherd's Purse after we learned all the parts, and Teacher said it was splendid. This is what it looks like.

This is a sketch
of a trembling
aspen tree. We
learned about it
in Botany last
week. I love
the shape of
the leaves. It
should be called
a trembling
heart tree.

Trembling Aspen

Mama says that a facility in Sketching is a desirable Achievement, especially on journeys, because that way you can record the scenery and share it with others.

Here is a
buttercup. I think
it looks splendid.

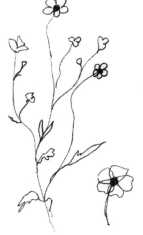

Wednesday, November 22

Here is a sketch of Mr. Onderdonk's Locomotive No. 2. Its name is Emory but everyone calls it Curly.

Not so splendid. I need to practise locomotives or stick to Botany. I think I will stick to words, at least in my Diary. And perhaps I should be more careful about what I say. But then, what is the use of having a Diary? Where else can I express Private Thoughts and Feelings?

Today in Penmanship we wrote:

Trials and troubles turn with time and tide.

I think that is another way of saying that things will get better, but it is not true. Here is my version:

Trials and troubles never turn or terminate.

Thursday, November 23

Thank goodness Papa will be home tomorrow. Then I know he'll be safe for a little while. I never had nightmares in Ottawa. Mama says that is because the Pacific Section of the railway is the most difficult and the most dangerous.

After school today I ironed shirts, dresses, linens and handkerchiefs and for once I did not scorch One Single Item. Mama was pleased.

Friday, November 24

Papa is home, safe and sound, with good news. The Skuzzy Creek Bridge is finished! But now he has to start on the Salmon River Bridge, 35 miles above Yale. He had some bad news, too — more accidents. This time two Chinese were hurt in a rock slide.

Mama says the Accident Hospital is bursting at the seams, but only with Whites. The Chinese are not allowed in, even though they're working for the railway, too.

Papa said that when white workers are injured, the Hospital will be of little use if the injured men cannot get there in time. He was probably thinking of the man who died a while ago. A blast went off and there was falling rock and his leg was cut off. He died because they could not get him to the Hospital soon enough.

I told Papa about my nightmares. He said I shouldn't worry because he thinks about me all the time and that makes him extra careful. But I am to pray for his safety nonetheless.

He says that most of the accidents happen when there is blasting. So I think they should have a doctor close by. And I think the doctors should stay put, not go off enjoying themselves or treating patients in town. Naturally no one asks for my opinion.

That must be the best part about being a reporter. You can state your opinions — once you have developed Thick Skin — whether anyone wants to hear them or not. There is bound to be *one* person in the world who would agree with you. As for the rest, you could try to change their minds.

I think I will be a reporter after all.

Saturday, November 25

Rain and mud. I feel very glum. Mama tells me I am experiencing nothing more serious than growing pains, and my glumness will not last forever. Easy for her to say, all grown up without a care in the world.

She suggested I go for an outing with Anne. I didn't tell her that Anne refuses to talk to me.

Oh, misery.

Later

Hurray! The Express coach has just arrived with mail and I got a letter from Rachel. Her mother is taking her to Victoria in January and they are stopping in Yale for 2 days, Jan. 3 to 5. But before that, I am invited to Aspen Hill Farm from December 27 to 29 "so we can give the horses a good canter" before she goes away.

I am so happy. Mama says she could light a candle with the glow on my face.

Sunday, November 26

Rain. Mud. Church.

I desperately want to ask Mama *when* they're sending me to Angela College. In the New Year, so I can go with Rachel? Or next fall? I am afraid to bring up the subject because then she will know I've been listening at doors. I would much rather keep that a Secret.

Papa went back to camp directly after Church. Why couldn't he run a newspaper like Mr. Hagan? Or be a butcher like Rusty's father? Then he could stay at home and be here every single night, safe with us.

Wednesday, November 29

School the same.

Chores the same.

Weather the same. Rain and Mud.

But today I marked Papa's finished bridge on Mr. Hagan's map!

Thursday, November 30

In Penmanship today we had another line that could be about the Fraser:

Rushing rapids roar round rising rivers.

It could be part of a poem, it is that stirring. Here's my own:

Roaring railways rush round rising rapids.

Or: *Rapid railways roar round rushing rivers.*

Sometimes I wonder if Teacher chooses our Penmanship lines with Yale in mind. I suppose not, because otherwise we would be penmanshipping nothing but trains and railways and we have not had a single one of those.

Is "penmanshipping" a word? It should be.

Monday, December 4

Melissa has taken a shine to me and follows me about like a puppy. I do not mind. I secretly pretend she is my little sister. At least I have someone to talk to, since Anne is still giving me the cold shoulder. How anyone can hold a grudge for so long is beyond my understanding.

At lunch I gave Melissa a doll I made from a railway spike. I glued on a face, braided some yarn for hair and found a scrap of green cotton for a dress. Melissa was thrilled and named the doll Katie.

I was pleased as punch — until Toby Big Ears said

it was a perfect name since the doll looked just like me.

Fury! Just because the doll is long and skinny and has brown hair and a green cotton dress. I should have used blue yarn and a scrap of flannel from Toby's nightshirt.

I was about to cuff him when Melissa said, "I know she looks like Katie and that's why I love her the best of all my dolls."

It is a relief to know that someone likes me.

Wednesday, December 6

Penmanship today:
By being busy boys become better.
HA!

Thursday, December 7

Thanks to Melissa, I now know why Anne has been avoiding me. Here is what happened.

This afternoon, Teacher told us a panther had been spotted on the Wagon Road between town and the Powder Works Factory and everyone going home that way should keep together and make a lot of noise. Melissa was scared — she lives right next door to the Powder Works — and asked me to walk her home. So I did.

On the way she asked me if I gave her the spike

doll because yesterday was her birthday. I was surprised — I didn't know it was her birthday. She told me she is having a party on Saturday but only Primary girls are invited. She wanted to invite me anyway, but Anne's sister, Charlotte, told her I didn't like birthday parties. And the reason she thought that is because I didn't go to Anne's. Even tho' I was Anne's Best Friend.

Well, I felt as if someone had kicked me in the stomach. I have been re-reading my Diary and the words don't lie — they show me I am a thoughtless beast. I didn't have to go to Rachel's the day of Anne's party, I could have waited for another time. I certainly could have shown some Regret — instead of giving Anne the impression that Rachel would be much more fun. And before I left for Spuzzum, did I give Anne a present? A birthday card? Did I wish her a happy birthday? Did I ask her one single thing about her party when I came back? No, no, no, no.

I do not deserve to have a friend.

Friday, December 8

Thank goodness, Anne is talking to me again.

I got up very early this morning and made Anne a railway spike doll. Then I wrote a little card and pinned it to the doll's dress. The note said:

Dear Anne, I am deeply sorry for hurting your feelings.

I hope you had a Happy Birthday. Can we still be friends? Yours truly, Kate.

I worried all the way to school. What if I was wrong? What if Anne was still mad about the jade, and the birthday had nothing to do with it?

My worries were for naught. Anne said she had been planning to write me a letter because she sorely missed having me for a friend.

Tomorrow we are going to spend the day together.

Saturday, December 9

Anne and I took our spike dolls to Melissa's and put on a puppet show for her party. There were eight little girls there, plus Melissa's brothers, and everyone loved it. "Katie" and "Annie" — our puppets — talked in funny voices and made jokes and even got into a fight! *Clang, clang, ring, ring* — it sounded as though a railway gang was working inside the house.

Then we changed our puppets' names to boys' names, like Toby and Rusty and Teacher — in dresses! with long plaits! — everyone laughed even harder.

Now I have to stop writing because my wrist is sore. Railway spikes are heavy!

Went to the *Sentinel* after school and Mr. Hagan let me set the type for a headline. It is a very difficult task because every letter has to go in backwards. So *b* looks like *d* and *d* looks like *b* and so forth. I took the letters from the type case, one by one, and arranged them in a small metal tray called a stick. I also put in space bars between the words.

The next step was moving my line of type to a larger metal tray called a galley. I had to be careful because if I dropped it, all the pieces of type would be mixed up. After that, I inked it. This is how the letters looked:

OOᗺIЯАɔ ƎHT
ᗡAOЯ ИOƆAW

Some letters look the same backwards and forwards, like *o*, *i*, *l*, *v*, *w*. They are my favourites.

Mr. Hagan gave me a sheet of paper and had me print the headline to *prove* I had not made any mistakes. Then he let me bring home my galley *proof*. Here it is:

THE CARIBOO
WAGON ROAD

It is a dull headline, but in a few days everyone will read it in the *Sentinel*, thanks to me.

I wonder if Mr. Hagan has nightmares about the *Sentinel* being printed backwards. Everyone would have to read the news in a mirror!

Wednesday, December 13

Cleaned the range after supper. Grim, hateful and least favourite chore. Mix the black lead with a drop of turpentine, apply it to the iron surfaces with a soft brush, rub vigorously with a stiff brush and give a final polish with a clean cloth. And Mama is so particular. Mercy McGinnis! You could use the surface as a mirror, it is already that shiny. You could use it to read a backwards *Sentinel*! And stay warm at the same time.

Saturday, December 16

Dark days of winter. Even when it is sunny we are in shadow most of the time, because of the high mountains. The days are getting shorter but they sometimes feel very long.

Monday, December 18

I like to imagine I'm as brave as a Knight but I have no more courage than a thistle. I'm afraid of doctors and dentists and bears and panthers and being adrift on the Fraser or on the Pacific Ocean. And I'm afraid of Fire, like the terrible one we had in August '81, even worse than the one in 1880.

My biggest fear at the moment is the Public Examination. An Examiner comes to school and asks questions to see how much we know. The questions can be about Reading, Spelling, Grammar, History, Geography, Arithmetic, Latin — anything that we study in school — and when our name is called we have to stand up and answer — in front of everyone, for the whole entire town is invited. Then the Examiner writes a report and Mr. Hagan prints it in the *Sentinel* for all the world to see.

The very thought of the Examination makes my knees shake, my heart pound and my stomach churn. Last year I could not speak without a stammer and I only answered half the questions correctly. Not because I did not know the answers, but because the Examiner frightened me witless. I would rather go to the dentist than go through that again. Alas, I have no choice. And it is only 4 days away.

Friday, December 22

The Examination was a torture — but it is over and I am still alive.

Great Godfrey, the ordeal had me trembling so hard I could scarcely breathe, let alone speak, and the Examiner kept saying, "Speak up, Miss," which made me tremble even more. I managed to spell *proficiency* correctly, and I conjugated a Latin verb, and named all the countries in the British Empire. I gave the correct definitions of several words, like *excruciating* (agonizing) and *petulant* (peevish) but I was hopeless at Mental Arithmetic, even though I've been practising. And the Kings that ruled during the Hundred Years War flew completely out of my mind.

Why couldn't the Examiner ask me about grasshopper trestles? Or how long it took the railway to blast the first four tunnels out of Yale? (18 months! No wonder our heads ached.)

Toby did poorly at Reading. But in Mental Arithmetic he did better than any of the seniors, including Andrew.

Andrew had to recite the first ten stanzas of "The Rime of the Ancient Mariner" and only stumbled on three lines.

I half hoped the Examiner would ask me to recite some lines. I would have launched into "The Song of the Locomotive" — *Beware! Beware! for I come in my might! With a scream, and a scowl of scorn,* etc. — but as I was so nervous, I'm sure I would not have done the poem justice.

The Examiner complimented us on our singing, especially when we sang "God Save the Queen." He also told us we were an intelligent class, exceedingly neat in appearance, and Attentive and Orderly throughout the day. Teacher's right eyebrow shot up with his smile.

Mama says she is proud of me and my brothers, and Papa will be, too.

Saturday, December 23

Bright blue sky — until the sun dipped below the mountains. But it was still a glorious day because our whole family went off to find a Christmas tree! Had a grand time tramping through the woods and up to our favourite spot in the mountains. Built a fire and ate our lunch and cut down a splendid Fir.

Sunday, December 24

Soft snow on the ground — perfect for Christmas.

Our tree looks beautiful. It is lit with Chinese lanterns that Mama got from Kwong Lee's store, and hundreds of candles. It also has tiny globes wrapped with sparkling tinsel.

Monday, December 25

Christmas Day, 1882

As soon as we got up we opened our stockings and presents. Mama loved the arrangement of dried flowers I made for her. She couldn't believe I picked the flowers in September and kept it a secret all this time.

We went to Church for Christmas service, then came home for Christmas dinner. I got the horse-shoe in my plum pudding! So I will have good luck in the coming year. Papa got the thimble and we all laughed — as if he could ever be an Old Maid.

Social calls all afternoon and evening and we played my favourite game, Snapdragon! First you put raisins and currants in a bowl and pour brandy over top so they soak. Then you put the bowl in the centre of the table, put out the lights, and set the brandy on fire. Everyone takes turns trying to snatch a piece of flaming fruit, and then they pop it into their mouth. Anne said it looked dangerous and she did not want to play, but she changed her mind when Andrew told her that the flames from burning brandy are not very hot.

We played for a long time and it was great fun. We sang the song, too. This is my favorite verse:

With his blue and lapping tongue
Many of you will be stung,
Snip! Snap! Dragon!

Now it is late and everyone has gone home. My tooth hurts something fierce because when I was eating the plum pudding I accidentally bit down hard on the horseshoe. Every Christmas Mama warns us to be careful. Oh, the PAIN! The horseshoe was meant to bring *good* luck.

Tuesday, December 26

Boxing Day

I am in a foul temper. My toothache kept me awake all night long and when I managed to catch a few winks, I dreamed about dentists. Which was enough to wake me up in even greater pain.

The very thought of being stuck in the dentist's chair makes me ill — trapped by a blood-stained spittoon on one side, a stand of torture instruments on the other, and the dentist looming over me in his rumpled white coat. I HATE dentists! Not only do they put you through the most excruciating Torture, they lie about it. I went twice to the dentist in Ottawa, and both times he told me it would not hurt, just a little pinch, and not even that much if I sat very brave and still. NOT TRUE! It hurt so frightfully I wanted to bite his thumb. But since my mouth was full of files and crowbars and pincers and chisels and goodness knows what else, crochet hooks and darning needles from the look of it — as well as his fingers and bloody bits of cotton — I could scarcely breathe, let alone bite. But I could kick! And kick I did, much to Mama's shame and disgrace when the dentist told her about my behaviour.

That was in Ottawa, but the dentist who comes to Yale is just as horrid, according to the stories I've heard, so no matter how bad the pain gets, I'm resolved NOT to tell Mama. I would rather yank out the tooth myself than go to the dentist.

Now I have to stop writing because we are going to the Institute Hall to see the Yale Amateur Minstrels. I hope the show takes my mind off the pain.

Later

Just got home from the Minstrel Show — 2 hours of songs and conundrums, stories and jokes. I did not enjoy it. In fact, I did not laugh once, not even in the sketch called "Love in Kentucky," which had the audience practically rolling on the floor. My whole being ached from tip to toe. How can one little tooth cause such excruciating misery?

Ex*tooth*iating misery — that could be the answer

to a conundrum. If I were not feeling so poorly, I would think of a question to go with it.

Wednesday, December 27

I am plagued by Bad Luck. I was supposed to go to Rachel's today but I can't because the Wagon Road is in such a state. Everyone blames the railway and says they have to repair it. I don't give two figs who fixes the road, I only want it fixed once and for all.

Andrew said I might as well get used to it because once the railway is finished, the road will be completely neglected and end up in ruins.

Toby asked Andrew when *he* became the expert, and then they were at it, hammer and tongs.

I asked Mama why I could not take my chances like everyone else who travels the road. She said because it is dangerous and there are too many accidents. Papa said I could go as soon as the road is in good repair. I said, "When will that be? The next time the Governor General comes to visit?"

The way I spoke made Mama cross. "Enough of that cheek, young lady!" she said.

I apologized.

Papa said that life is full of Disappointments.

Hell's Gate and Goblins! I do not like it one bit. Now my toothache is worse. And it rained the whole livelong day.

Thursday, December 28

No use hiding anything from Mama. She wrapped cotton around a darning needle, dipped it in oil of cloves and told me to hold it against my tooth to ease the pain. It helped for a while, enough for me to go to the carol sing at Church. Rusty said I smelled like gingerbread.

After the carol sing, Anne and I went to her father's Chemist Shop and we discovered millions of cures for coughs and cleansing the blood and what have you, but not one easy cure for toothache. Only the dentist. Mama said I will have to see him the moment he is back in Yale.

Friday, December 29

I missed my journey to Spuzzum but at least Rachel will be here in 5 days. I hope my toothache is better by then. It is *not* better today.

Mama decided to try creosote instead of oil of cloves. It smells like soot and burns if it touches my mouth or skin, but as soon as it is pressed against my tooth, the pain goes away. Why can't it stay away? Toby offered to pull out the wretched tooth but I'm afraid he would pull the wrong one.

Life is unfair.

Monday, January 1st, 1883

NOT a Happy New Year. Rain. Toothache. Chores — but I only had to feed the chickens, since Mama is taking pity.

We had visitors coming and going all day long for Auld Lang Syne and New Year's punch but I didn't enjoy a single minute.

I'm feeling very cross and sorry for myself. Everyone knows a cure for toothache but nothing works. Mr. Harrison told me there is nothing better than smoking a pipe of tobacco and caraway seeds.

Anne has a Book of Saints and said I could try praying to Saint Apollonia, the patron saint of toothache sufferers.

And Rusty! He told me he had a sure-fire cure for toothache. He gave me a shilling from his coin collection and a thin piece of sheet zinc and told me to hold the aching tooth between the zinc and silver because the zinc and silver act as a sort of battery and create enough electricity to establish a current and so relieve the pain.

Toby Big Ears said he remembered reading about that in a *Boy's Own Paper* — one of the ones I had given to the Library. And Rusty said that is where he read it, in the Library, so it must have been Toby's paper.

Then Toby asked Rusty if he wanted to see the

new papers he had received for Christmas and off they went — leaving poor me with the electrical cure. "The pain will be gone by magic." Ha! It did not work.

Mrs. Murray's suggestion sounded the nicest, a few drops of friar's balsam on cotton. Mama says the end result would be no different than creosote. I greatly prefer the name *friar's balsam*, but unfortunately there is none at hand.

Mama has just given me some syrup — not Squill's, but Mrs. Winslow's Soothing Syrup. I'm starting to feel very drowsy.

Tuesday, January 2

Dreadful news!

Mama told me that since the dentist will not be back in Yale until February, I'll have to see the dentist in New Westminster. So Papa is taking me on the boat first thing tomorrow. *Tomorrow*! I pleaded and sobbed — not tomorrow! I'll miss seeing Rachel!

My pleas fell on deaf ears. I could have asked more politely, I suppose, but my toothache is venting my spleen and putting me in an exceedingly bad temper.

Toby asked if I'm planning to kick the dentist this time, the cheek. I kicked him instead.

Mama has just given me some more of Mrs.

Winslow's Soothing Syrup to help me sleep. Good. I hope I never wake up — unless the weather turns cold overnight. Because if there is ice on the Fraser, the stern-wheeler will not run.

Monday, January 8, 11 A.M.

I'm home. And since I did not take my Diary to New Westminster, here is a full account of My Adventurous Journey.

Wednesday, Jan. 3 — No ice on the river so the boat left Yale as usual, with poor me on it. I scarcely remember the trip to New Westminster because Papa gave me Soothing Syrup and I slept the whole way. Spent the night in a hotel.

Thursday, Jan. 4 — The dentist was what I expected, right down to the little steel files and crowbars. In the middle of the torture, the tooth broke apart. The dentist kept telling me to keep still, he had to dig it out, but I could not help but squirm and struggle, and finally he put some foul-smelling cotton over my face and that is all I remember.

The next thing I knew I was back at the hotel with Papa. I felt wretched all over — swollen jaw, throbbing gums, headache, nausea. I wanted to vomit and I did. Papa said it was the effects of the chloroform — what the dentist used to put me to sleep — and it would wear off. He called me a Brave Little Puss. I did not feel brave, only sick.

Friday, Jan. 5 — Snowed overnight. In the morning we boarded the *Wm. Irving* and left New Westminster — Papa, me and a score of other passengers. Arrived at Harrison River where we were supposed to board the *Reliance* because the water level in the Fraser was too low for the *Wm. Irving*. But the *Reliance* was not there. We waited and waited and it got later and later. Then we learned that the *Reliance* was stuck on a bar about 4 miles farther up the river.

Our captain decided to go to the rescue. But he could not go until morning, because the current was too fast and dangerous in the dark. So they tied up the *Wm. Irving* and we spent the night on board. I was thankful that Mama had made me wear my fur coat, so I was not as cold as some. Papa was wearing his fur coat, too.

Saturday, Jan. 6 — The *Reliance* captain came over in a canoe, and some Indians, too. There was ice floating all around but they managed to attach a cable between the two steamers, then tried to pull the *Reliance* off the bar. The first time they tried, the line broke. Then it broke again. And again. We might as well have been on the *Skuzzy*.

Spent another cold night on board.

Sunday, Jan. 7 — Intense cold. Saw the sun rise over the mountain but no warmth came through.

The Captains tried again and the line broke. So they finally gave up and all the passengers from the *Reliance* got into the canoe and came aboard our boat. Then we went back to Harrison River and got off the boat. Everyone was ill-tempered.

Papa said all would be well because the railway track was laid to within 3 miles of Harrison River and — if we moved smartly — the engine and cars could take us to Yale that same evening.

So off we went, trudging smartly through the snow. Some of the bridges were unfinished so we had to walk single file over the icy timbers. Papa offered to carry me but I managed on my own — though my heart was in my stomach the whole entire time.

We reached Farr's Bluff in the middle of no-where, not a house in sight, dark as pitch, but thank goodness, the engine was there. The conductor waved his lantern and helped us climb onto the flatcar. It had been carrying gravel to ballast the road and it was full of dirt, snow and ice. There was no other choice, so that is where we had to ride. Most of the passengers were grumpy, but I snuggled up against Papa and did not feel too bad.

The Conductor told us that the train had run off the track four times that day, and to make sure it did not happen a fifth time, they were going to run the train very slowly. This made the passengers even more grumpy.

We started off about 7 P.M. I was exceedingly tired, but whenever I fell asleep, something would jolt me awake. The wind howled, the bridges creaked. I was afraid they might collapse altogether.

We stopped at Hope Station and some passengers got off. We carried on. In the first tunnel above Hope an icicle hit the rail with so much force I thought the echo alone would cause the tunnel to cave in over our heads. When the engine passed through the east end of the tunnel we heard a crash and breaking glass and later learned that the engine's cab had been smashed by several icicles and the fireman got cuts all over his head and face. Then a huge icicle fell and hit the man sitting beside me. His leg was sorely injured. So it was a narrow escape for me.

Monday, Jan. 8 — We got to Emory just after midnight. Everything was fine after Emory until we got to the first cut below Yale and the engine got stuck in a snowdrift. The engineer backed down and got up some more steam for a second try. As we were ploughing through the snowdrift, a wheel went off the rail and jumped over half a dozen ties. My body rattled tooth, nail and bone, but finally we got back on the tracks.

We reached Yale at 2 oClock this morning, the latest I've been up in my entire life. I wanted to wake my brothers and tell them everything, but I must have been more exhausted than I thought, for the moment I saw Mama I flung myself into her arms and burst into tears. She gave me some hot cocoa and tucked me into bed and I went straight to sleep.

So that is the account of my Journey. I think I did a fair job of keeping eyes and ears open, all things considered. It has taken me a good hour to write the account and my hand is somewhat cramped. No matter, since every part of my body aches anyway after being battered about for days. Especially my jawbone, thanks to the rough handling of the dentist. But the offending tooth is gone. Hip, hip, hurray! I am exceedingly thankful.

Mama let me sleep through the morning and now I think it is time for lunch.

Still Monday, 2 P.M.

I have just finished lunch. I was hungry enough to eat a wolf but happily settled for hashed venison with red-currant jelly and mashed potatoes, and for sweet I had two slices of Tipsy Cake. The cake was well soaked in sherry and brandy and smelled deliciously like plum pudding (but without the fruit). Mama made the custard with 8 eggs instead of 5 and put in extra almonds. She said I deserved a Treat!

The house is quiet because Toby and Andrew are at school. I'm sorry I missed school, especially today, for it is the first day back after holidays and everyone will have stories to tell. I can't wait to tell Anne and Rusty about my journey.

I'm sad about missing Rachel.

My tongue is driving me to distraction, poking into the hole in my gum as if it wonders where the tooth has gone.

A dreadful thought — when I smile, will people notice the gaping hole in my mouth? It feels as big as a boulder.

Relief! I just smiled into the mirror and the same Kate smiled back, not a toothless hag.

Tuesday, January 9

KATE IS A PIG-HEADED FOOL!

Anne had no interest in hearing about my Adventure because she had something to tell me which — in her opinion — was far more important. "Remember when Margaret and Mary Stout gave the Governor General the gold specimens?" she said.

She went on to tell me that they each received a book in the mail, signed from Princess Louise and the Governor General. Then she said that if it had not been for me, we would have given them the jade and received a book, too.

Could she leave it at that? No! All day long, "Imagine, having a book signed from Princess Louise." And, "What a treasure." And, "The Stouts are so lucky." On and on till I wanted to scream. She told me Margaret's book is called *Our Little Ones* and Mary's is *Papa's Little Daughters* and they are both beautifully illustrated.

Andrew told me I could mail the Princess the jade if it is that important. I know I could, but it would not be the same.

I wonder what book Princess Louise would have chosen for me, had I not been such a peevish, pig-headed fool.

Wednesday, January 10

I've been saving my pennies and finally have a quarter. Now I can buy *Grip's Comic Almanac* for 1883. I've seen it in the Stationers and it is even better than last year's, full of fun and pictures. I'm going to buy one and give it to Toby for his birthday this weekend. I know he will be pleased. And I'm sure he will let me read it. Even though he is still angry at me for donating all our other almanacs to the library. At least I got them back. Is *undonate* a word? Mr. Harrison was understanding and said my heart was in the right place.

Thursday, January 11

Cold!! Three degrees below freezing and the wind is blowing enough to shave a mouse.

Another cold-shoulder day from Anne.

Saturday, January 13

Toby's 14th birthday. Mama and Papa gave him new skates so we went skating on the pond out by the Powder Works Factory.

Rusty was there. He waved and skated toward me but stumbled and fell. I felt embarrassed for him, especially when Finch laughed.

The whole time we were skating my stomach took funny turns. I won't tell Mama. She would make me take more cod liver oil.

In the afternoon I helped Mama make a cake for Toby and decorated it myself, with peppermint frosting. Toby loved it. He also loved the *Almanac* and said I could read it. But if I gave it to the Library he would have my head.

Thursday, January 18

Went sledding after school with Toby. Rusty and Clara wanted to come but they had to go home and milk the cows. Andrew said he wanted to do some reading — very unusual for Andrew.

I wanted to ask Anne but I am afraid she is still angry with me. I wish I had never thought of giving Princess Louise the jade — it has caused nothing but trouble.

Lots of ice going downriver. Toby says there might be a jam farther down.

No boats, no mail. I wonder if Rachel is enjoying Angela College.

Friday, January 19

I have been thinking long and hard. And today I swallowed my pig-headedness and told Anne she was right. I was petulant and selfish and she had every reason to be angry. Especially since the jade was meant to be a gift from her as well as from me. So I said, "Why don't we wrap it up and mail it to Princess Louise?" Because Anne is right, a signed book from a Princess would be everlastingly special.

Well, lo and behold — Anne told me it was not that important after all. She said she was sorry she hurt my feelings by going on and on about it and she hoped we could still be Best Friends. I said we could.

After school I went to her house for hot cocoa and told her all about my Adventure coming home from the dentist. Then we played Parcheesi. We both agreed that the books sent to the Stout girls sounded rather dull.

Saturday, January 20

Frightful day. Went sledding with Toby and Andrew — Andrew tore himself away from his books — and when it was time to come home we took a shortcut through the woods and found a man lying in the snow. He was as stiff as a board and I thought he was dead. Toby found bottles scattered about and Andrew said the man was alive but unconscious from drink. We could not leave him there or he would freeze to death, so we put him on the sled and dragged him into town.

Goodness, he was heavy. Sometimes he woke up and shouted for the snakes to get out of his eyes. Andrew said he had the DTs — whatever that means.

Constable Lewis spotted us by the tracks and said he would look after the man. So we came home. I still feel a little shaky. Who was the man? Where did he come from?

Monday, January 22

The man we rescued was put in jail but he is not a criminal — he had nowhere else to go. He used to work for the railway. Both his feet got frozen and this morning he was taken to the hospital in New Westminster to get them amputated.

Constable Lewis told us it was a good thing we came along when we did or it would have been worse.

Toby asked if we might get a Reward for saving his life. The cheek. I hope he felt ashamed when Constable Lewis said no, the man was destitute.

How will he manage without his feet? The thought is too gruesome and sad. Constable Lewis said he would likely go home to California.

Andrew told me DT stands for *delirium tremens*. I know what that means from my Latin: Trembling delirium.

I do not understand about the snakes.

Destitute: suffering extreme want.

Thursday, January 25

More snow. Good sleighing.

The mail finally came through with a parcel from Grandma Forrest. Three birthday presents — one for Toby, one for Andrew and one for me. I wish England were closer. Our presents always arrive too early or too late. Eventually they do arrive, and for that I am thankful.

Saturday, January 27

Washed hair — and it is still not dry, even though I've been brushing it by the fire for what seems like half a day.

Once a fortnight is far too frequent for this chore. Wash with borax and olive oil, rinse in cold water, apply two egg yolks and rinse again. What an ordeal! Mama says I'll be thankful one day, as my hair is my most attractive feature.

I think not. It is too long and thick and wavy and brown — brunette, says Mama — and it has an unruly mind of its own. Why can't it be straight and fair like Anne's?

I read an article in *Girl's Own Paper* that says "the secret to having a good head of hair is to cultivate a calm and unruffled frame of mind." If this is true, I must surely be the exception.

Saturday, February 3

I love it when Papa is home. Last night we played Charades and Parcheesi and cracked nuts by the fire.

This morning he told us the railway news — six Chinese workers died at Camp 14, from scurvy. When I asked why they did not go to the Hospital before it was too late, he reminded me that the Hospital is only for *accidents*. Even if *white* railway workers are sick they can't go into the Yale Hospital. But they can go to the one in Lytton. He also told us that seven more Chinese died below Hope.

Toby said, "You mean they were beyond hope?"

He meant it as a joke but it wasn't funny and nobody laughed.

After lunch, Papa went to visit Mr. Hagan. He tells him the railway news so it gets printed in Thursday's *Sentinel*. Sometimes when I help Mr. Hagan set the type I see the news I already know.

Wednesday, February 7

On Sunday Papa went back to work but he is home again already! He says it is too stormy and cold for railway work — the Chinese workers stay inside their tents and the engines can't run because of the snow and ice on the rails.

I think it is too stormy and cold for *anything*. The wind could shave a bear let alone a mouse. At least our house is cozy, especially since Papa and Andrew filled the cracks around the windows. Now the wind can whistle all it likes. It can't get inside.

Thursday, February 8

Here is a riddle I read in the *Sentinel*:

Why are young ladies at the breaking up of a party like arrows?

Because they can't go off without a beau and are in a quiver till they get one.

I told Papa I did not understand and he said I would soon enough. Which was NOT a helpful answer.

One week till my birthday.

Friday, February 9

I'm happy Papa is home. The Salmon River Bridge is even longer and higher than the last one.

Monday, February 12

Papa has gone again. Why couldn't he stay home until my birthday? I hate the railway. I wish they would get it finished once and for all.

Tuesday, February 13

Splendid day! Sunshine, sledding and a letter from Rachel. Tucked inside was a handkerchief she embroidered for my birthday. It has pink hearts and blue and yellow flowers in the corners. It is very fine

— even Mama was impressed. Rachel was all thumbs when it came to embroidery, even thumbier than me.

She told me all about Angela College and her new friends, and how much she misses her horse. So could I please go to the farm and give Fireweed a good fast canter and a kiss on the nose.

I hope I can. But sometimes Spuzzum seems as far away as Victoria. And Victoria might as well be in England.

Only 2 days until my birthday. I'll be thirteen.

Thursday, February 15, 1883

Today is my birthday — but it did not start out very nicely. Last night the water pipes froze all over town so everyone was out with buckets carrying water from the river, including me.

I had a wonderful birthday, once I finished hauling water. When I got to school, Anne gave me a white linen handkerchief like the one I received from Rachel, but instead of embroidery, she crocheted lace around the edges. I told Anne it was such a fine piece of work she should have sent it to Princess Louise instead of giving it to me. She looked very pleased.

Rusty gave me a card with a poem he wrote himself. It says:

The rose is red
The violets blue
Pinks are pretty
And so are you.

He blushed when he gave it to me and I must have blushed, too, for my face certainly felt hot. It feels hot just thinking about it. And it is almost the end of the day.

Andrew gave me a picture of a mountain that he made with pyrography and Grandma Forrest sent me a pretty thimble and a whole new set of *Girl's Own Papers*. Mama and Papa gave me a silver locket in the shape of a heart.

Toby gave me something unexpected — my jade rock! Cut in half and polished! He said he cut it with an axe — along with the tip of his thumb (a Toby Joke) — then polished the two cut edges with an emery board. It really looks like a precious stone now.

Mama made a cream cake with lemon frosting and I was just about to blow out my candles when in walked Papa. It was a perfect surprise.

Later

Now I have the biggest surprise of all. Mama just came in to kiss me good night and told me that come September, I'll have a new baby brother or sister. Please let it be a sister.

Friday, February 16

Mama told me that I will soon be a woman and there are some things I should know. So she told me. But she can't have told me everything because I'm terribly confused. To go through the misery she described, every month for years and years and years? The thought is unbearable. I refuse to write another word about it. Not even when the dreaded event takes place.

I wish I could have stayed twelve forever. I'm certain that Rachel feels the same, although she has been thirteen since June and may be quite used to it by now. The next time I write I'll ask her how she feels.

Saturday, February 17

I cut out a piece from the *Sentinel* a while ago and I'm copying it into my Diary as a way of practising my Penmanship. Here it is. (A lady wrote it, not Mr. Hagan.)

Upon the whole, it is a dreadful bother to be a woman, and to do the business up in good shape.

In the first place, You've got to look well, or else you're nobody. A man may be homely, and still popular. Whiskers cover up most of his face, and if he has a large mouth nobody mistrusts it; and if he has wrinkles on his forehead, his friends speak of his many cares, and of his thoughtful disposition, and tell each other that his wrinkles are lines of thought. Lines of thought, indeed, when in all probability his forehead is wrinkled by the habit he has of scowling at his wife when the coffee isn't strong enough.

Papa never scowls at Mama.

A woman can't go out alone, because she must be protected. She can't go anywhere when it rains, because her hair won't stay crimped

What is crimped hair? If I had crimped hair would I still have to wash it once a fortnight in egg yolks?

and she will get mud on her petticoats and things. She can't be a Free Mason, because she would tell their secrets and everybody would know about that goat and that gridiron.

Goat and gridiron? I do not understand. Now my fingers have writing cramps so I'll finish another time.

Sunday, February 18

Church.
Roast beef and Yorkshire pudding for dinner — and I made the Yorkshire pudding. It was done to a

turn, although a little too brown on top. But nobody scowled.

Here is some more about being a woman:

She can't smoke because it wouldn't be feminine.

Who would want to? Toby dared me once and I did and it made me sick.

She can't go courting, because it is unwomanly. But she must get married before 30, or people will sigh and wonder why the men don't seem to take, and all the old maids and widows will smile significantly and keep quiet.

Why do they smile *significantly*?

It is everybody's business who a woman marries. They put their heads together and talk over the pros and cons and decide whether she is good enough for him. And they criticize the shape of her nose and the way she does up her hair and relate how lazy her grandfather was and how her Aunt Sally sold beans and buttermilk.

I love buttermilk. What is the harm in selling it?

A woman must wear No. 2 boots on No. 3 feet, and she must manage to dress well on seventy-five cents a week; she mustn't be vain and she must be kind to the poor, and go regularly to the sewing society meetings, and be ready to dress dolls, make aprons and tidies for church fairs.

Mama does all that (except for wearing under-sized boots) and helps at the Accident Hospital. Altho' she is not helping quite so much any more because of the Baby.

She must hold herself in continual readiness to find everything her husband has lost — and a man never knows where anything is. He will put his boots away on the parlour sofa, and when he has hunted for them half an hour he will appear to his wife with a countenance like that of an avenging angel and demand to know "What she has done with his boots?"

Just like my brothers.

She must shut all the doors after her lord and master, and likewise the bureau drawers, for a married man was never known to shut a drawer. It would be as natural for a hen to go in swimming for recreation.

We might go on indefinitely with the troubles being a woman brings; and if there is a man in the world who thinks that a woman has an easy time of it, why just let him pin a pound of false hair to his head, and get inside a new pair of corsets and put on a pull-back overskirt, and be a woman himself, and see how he likes it.

Great Galoshes, I'd like to see Papa try. Or my brothers.

Thursday, February 22

The snow is disappearing. We are back to rain and dark, gloomy weather, like my mood. At least the water is running in the pipes again. No more Bucket Brigades to the river.

I'm exceedingly sad about Rachel being in Victoria. I may never see her again. Mama says of course I'll see her, she has not moved away for good, her parents are still in Spuzzum so she'll be back for holidays and Victoria is not the end of the Earth, we can write letters, we will always be friends, and so on. But it won't be like that, I know it won't, because the same thing happened the time I left Ottawa and the time before that when we moved from Toronto. I hate moving away and leaving my friends, and I hate it when my friends do the same. It is not fair.

I told Mama we are like corks on the water, tossed about higgledy-piggledy by the whims of our parents and the wretched railway. She merely smiled and told me I was being melodramatic. At that I burst into tears and came up to my room. She never takes me seriously.

Friday, February 23

Today Mama said she understands how I feel because once upon a time she was my age. She said that life does not always turn out the way you want it to, but I'll make many new friends — like Anne, for instance — and it is all right to have a good cry. Then she made me a cup of tea.

I felt the time had come. While we were having our tea, I told her that I would like to go to Angela College after all. She said, "Angela College? We were never planning to send you to Angela College. Wherever did you get that idea?"

So I told her. She said I had taken a few words out of context and created a story that wasn't true — a perfect example of why one should never listen in on conversations. LESSON LEARNED.

She admitted that she and Papa had once thought of sending me to a girls' school in England — the same one she had attended — but they could not afford the cost. As for Angela College, they had known for some time that Rachel's parents were sending her there. The conversation I'd overheard might have been the time they were talking about Rachel and wondering how she would manage at the College, being "as wild as Kate," and how it would take some doing to turn Rachel into a lady.

So there it is, and what a fine kettle of fish. I leap before I look and jump to conclusions, all for naught. For months I've been agonizing over Angela College — first dreading, then anticipating — and wasting time on the mastery of Social Graces. I would have been better off learning pyrography. Or plunging deeper into Mental Arithmetic. ANOTHER LESSON LEARNED.

Mama told me she would never send me away, she would miss me too much. And she would certainly never send me away now, because she needs me at home. Because — and this is a revelation — because after my sisters died there were two other times when she was expecting a baby. And each time she lost the baby before it was even born. This time, she is counting on me to take over much of the cooking and cleaning so that she can rest and keep the Baby safe.

Now I'm weary of talk and revelations. I'm going to see if Toby wants a game of Checkers before bed.

Saturday, February 24

Papa is home with sad news — two *more* Chinese workers died from scurvy. The other day Mr. Hagan said it is dreadful that the railway does not take better care of them since it is the railway that brought them here. I mentioned this to Papa and he said there is nothing he can do, he is not in charge.

Then he said that some Chinese business people in Yale formed a society called the Benevolent

Society and they are going to open a hospital in Yale or somewhere on the railway line for the Chinese who get sick or injured.

Toby said he had heard about corpses floating down the river because the bodies were not properly buried. Papa said it was only a rumour.

I like the sound of the word, *benevolent*. It means doing good.

Monday, February 26

Finch fell through the ice and it serves him right. We were skating after school and Finch started a game of Red Rover, boys against the girls. Anne insisted we call *him* over so we did and he broke through our line and picked me. On the way back to the boys' side he gave me a push and I went flying off on my own.

There was a loud CRACK and everybody screamed and I turned around and Finch was in the pond. It is not a deep pond but he was soaked up to his waist. Good thing he pushed me on ahead or I would have gone down, too.

After that we came home and Mama made us hot cocoa. Rusty came over to read some *Boy's Own Paper*s with Toby, but he played Parcheesi with me instead. Toby played, too.

Tuesday, February 27

Rain. Snow slides. No more skating.

In school today I skipped ahead in my Reader and read all about the Taking of Quebec on the Plains of Abraham. Here is something I discovered about General Wolfe. As he prepared his men to attack the French, he recited lines from Gray's "Elegy in a Country Churchyard," one of the many English poems Mama compelled us to memorize during our period of home schooling. This is how the poem ends: *The paths of glory lead but to the grave.* It was truly prophetic because General Wolfe was killed on the battlefield. General Montcalm was mortally wounded and died the next day. But there is no mention of the poem he may have recited.

Wednesday, February 28

More snow slides today. They sound like explosives.

I wanted to help Mr. Hagan after school but Mama said it was high time I had a new coat. So off we tramped through mud and slush to Kwong Lee's because all the winter goods are on sale. Nothing fit and I was so cross — and then Rusty walked in, just as Mama was saying, "Katie, you're growing in *all* directions at once." HUMILIATION! Especially when Rusty smiled. I wanted to bury my head in ice.

Thursday, March 1

March is in like a lamb instead of a lion and the roads are drying up. Today I walked to school without squishing and sloshing.

Mama told me there is now a Chinese Hospital in Yale, set up in Sam Sing's house in Chinatown. He runs the laundry where Mama sometimes sends our washing.

I do not know how Mama can say I'm growing in all directions. Upwards, yes, but outwards? I'm still as flat as a flounder.

Friday, March 2

Mr. Hagan says a newspaperman must be objective and not allow his personal beliefs to colour what he reports. But he should practise what he preaches. This is what he said in last week's *Sentinel*:

Why no more interest is felt for the semi-slaves of China is somewhat surprising. No medical attention is furnished nor apparently much interest felt for these poor creatures. We understand Mr. Onderdonk declines interfering, while the Lee Chuck Co., that brought the Chinamen from their native land, refuses to become responsible for doctors and medicine. Surely some action should be taken by the locals, if not for the sake of the unfortunate

Chinamen themselves but for the protection of the white population.

Saturday, March 3

Four more Chinese died of scurvy.

Friday, March 9

Papa came home and I showed him what Mr. Hagan wrote. He said it is brave but foolhardy for Mr. Hagan to write such things. None of the other newspapers in the province would be so bold, for fear of losing their readers. He says no one wanted the Chinese to come, but everyone wants the railway. And the railway cannot be built without them.

Mama asked Papa what shape the Wagon Road is in and Papa said *bad* shape. But it would be in good order by spring and then he would take me to Aspen Hill Farm to give Fireweed a good gallop. I'd told him about Rachel's request weeks ago and he remembered. He said, "I'll take my favourite girl."

I know Papa spoils me a little but I never thought my brothers noticed, much less cared. When Papa comes home he always gives me a hug and says, "How is my favourite girl?" and my brothers either pay no attention or roll their eyes. But tonight Toby said something that hurt me to the bone. He said, "If the new baby's a girl, you won't be Papa's favourite."

His words hurt because I know he is right. How can a gangly, petulant, often bad-tempered 13-year-old ever compete with a baby?

Tuesday, March 13

Felt like summer all day today. Teacher said we'll be having our Botany lessons outdoors in no time. Sketching, too. Hurray!

Sunday, March 18

Mama said she will not be helping at the Hospital any more — not because the work tires her too much but because the Hospital is moving up the line, closer to where the railway work is going on. Toby is disappointed, the heartless ghoul.

Thursday, March 22

Helped Mama make hot cross buns. Tomorrow I am going up the hill to pick trilliums to decorate the church for Easter Sunday. Anne is coming with me. I hope it does not rain.

Good Friday, March 23

Today was an exceedingly Good Friday because I got a dog! Here is how it happened.

Anne and I went into the woods and picked all sorts of trilliums and different kinds of ferns. When our baskets were full, Anne went home but I stayed to cut some balsam fir.

Now here is the good part. On the way back I decided to take a different trail — to see if I could find some Pussy Willows — and as I was walking along I saw a man pulling a dog by a rope. The dog was whimpering something terrible, trying to break away, and the man was carrying a rifle. Well, I knew in an instant what he was planning to do. I dropped everything and yelled, "Don't shoot her!"

He stopped and said he had to shoot her because she was about to have pups and he had more than enough dogs already.

So I asked if I could have her.

"More fool you," he said and handed me the rope.

He warned me she was an ill-tempered mutt but I did not believe it. The moment I untied the rope she was bouncing all over me, licking my face and wagging her tail and yapping with the joy of being rescued. I gave her a hug and called her Sheba. She followed me home and even carried a branch of balsam.

Mama took one look at Sheba and said I could not keep her — she was going to have pups in a matter of days, and what would we do with pups?

Fortunately Papa was home. He said he would make a spot for Sheba under the house so she could have her pups and not be any trouble. Then we would see.

Sheba took to Toby and Andrew as readily as she took to me. Andrew said she looked like she had some Labrador Retriever in her, and maybe some Springer Spaniel, and she could be trained to be a good hunting dog for grouse and wild geese.

Papa said Andrew had a good point and even Mama looked at Sheba with a little more interest.

Saturday, March 24

Weather too fine for chores, but did them anyway. Then I went to Church to help with the Easter decorations. Everyone thanked me for the balsam fir because it smells so aromatic.

Went fishing with Toby in the afternoon. Andrew stayed home with his books, much to Toby's disappointment.

The creek was boiling with trout and we each caught three. Sheba came, too. She is not the least bit ill-tempered.

Almost time for my Saturday night bath. It is an ordeal, but not as wearisome as washing, rinsing, combing, untangling, drying and brushing and braiding my hair. Mama will not allow me to cut it

— it is long enough to sit on — and I can't pin it up for another three years. Misery.

March 25, 1883

Easter Sunday

The Church looked beautiful this morning, dressed up for Easter with jars of ferns and trilliums in every window, feathery moss and evergreens all over the altar and garlands of balsam fir.

When we came home from church we had the most wonderful surprise — Sheba has four puppies!

Friday, March 30

Such a muddled month. Now March is going *out* like a lion instead of a lamb. Today we had wind and rain and more snow. But the snow did not last.

A carpenter working on a bridge fell and broke his back and died. It wasn't Papa's bridge, but another one.

I still have nightmares about Papa being hurt. Sometimes he is on the stretcher and Toby is crying that he can see his brains.

I pray very, very hard that Papa will be safe.

Monday, April 16

Two weeks of cold, wet weather, school and chores.

I tried to knit a sweater for the Baby but kept dropping stitches, tried to embroider a bib but the threads got tangled, then tried to crochet lace around a handkerchief for Rachel. Every attempt was a *failure*.

Thank Goodness for Sheba's roly-poly puppies! They love to play tug-of-war with a bit of cloth, or chase after a ball.

The littlest one curls up in my lap while I'm doing schoolwork — if I can sneak her inside without Mama knowing! I call her Callie.

Tuesday, April 17

I went to the *Sentinel* today and looked at Mr. Hagan's map. When we first came to Yale, Mr. Onderdonk had the contract to build the railway from Emory to Yale and from Yale to Boston Bar. Now there are only a few miles left to go.

Mr. Onderdonk also got the contracts to build the railway through the upper part of the Canyon — from Boston Bar to Lytton, Lytton to Junction Flat, and Junction Flat to Savona's Ferry, which is very close to Kamloops. There are gangs working on all those sections, blasting and bridging and laying track, but Great Godfrey, will they ever be done?

Mr. Hagan showed me the Rocky Mountains and the Selkirk Mountains and told me the railway gangs in those sections are working just as hard as the gangs in the Pacific Section, and before long the tracks will meet. But no one knows exactly where.

Wednesday, April 18

A grisly day!

I woke to a caterwauling so terrible it set my teeth on edge and my nerves shivering up a storm. Got up and went downstairs — Mama, Toby and Andrew were already there — and Toby said there was a panther under the house! Andrew got his rifle and said he would shoot it but Mama would not let him go outside. The rest of the night we had to listen to the unearthly screaming, not knowing what was happening but fearing the worst — and unable to sleep.

In the morning everything was quiet. There was no screaming and no sign of the panther, but we found a hole going a little ways under the house and blood all over. We think that the panther was trying to get at the puppies but he could only squeeze in so far before Sheba attacked and forced him to back away. He kept trying and she kept attacking and that is why the panther was screaming all night long.

Mama got hold of two hunters and they came with their hounds and the hounds took the scent. Toby and Andrew went along on the hunt, but I stayed home with Sheba. Poor, brave Sheba! She made it through the ordeal with only a scratch but what a time she had. At least her puppies are all safe.

The hunters came back in a couple of hours with the *dead* panther. He was a good size — almost ten feet long from tip to tail, and chewed up something fierce, thanks to Sheba. It is actually a *good* thing he was so big. If he had been any smaller, he could have got all the way under the house and reached the puppies' hiding place.

Saturday, April 21

Today I went for a stroll with Anne along the Wagon Road toward Emory. We hoped we might have an Adventure but we did not — even though the Road goes right through the Powder Works with "Beware of Fire" signs at every turn. Not that I wanted a *fire* Adventure.

We had a cautious look around although we did not understand what all the buildings were about. There is the Chemical Works building — a big one with two storeys — and some buildings where they make nitro-glycerine and a Powder Magazine. I told Anne that was where I thought we had to live when we first came to Yale and she laughed.

We stopped in at the Foxes' and put on a puppet show for Melissa and her little brothers. This time we stuck pine cones on twigs and used leaves for the dresses. They were much lighter than railway spikes but they did not last long, especially in our vigorous fighting scenes. Mrs. Fox said we were more laughs than the Minstrel Show and should start selling tickets!

We tried dressing up Molly the cat, but all we got was scratches.

After we left the Foxes', we went to Clara's and helped milk the cows. We got more milk on our faces and clothing than in the bucket because Rusty was there and kept squirting us, the beast. Of course we squirted back. It was great fun.

Got home late and milky — but with a jar of thick, fresh cream. So Mama wasn't too cross.

Monday, April 23

Great Godfrey! Is there ever an end to Spring Cleaning? Mama says, "Heave-ho, Kate! A job worth doing is a job worth doing well."

But is this job worth doing? I do not mind a little dust or oil soot or mud, but Mama thinks otherwise.

Here are the chores for the coming week: wash all windows, mirrors and floors, pack winter clothes, polish furniture, scour walls, clean the pantry, clean the carpets, take down the winter drapes and put up the summer ones.

I would rather hammer spikes along the railway. At least I would be out of doors.

Thank Goodness it is time for bed. I hope Saturday never comes. That is the day we hang out the carpets and beat them black and blue — unless it rains. A hopeful thought.

Wednesday, April 25

Today the puppies started a new game — trying to chase Sheba! Round and round the chicken shed they stumbled, trying to catch her, but she was determined to have a rest. Then the rooster started chasing them! He looked so fierce and the puppies looked so funny, tripping over their big feet in their haste to scamper away.

I watched while I was washing the kitchen windows and it made the chore much more enjoyable.

Friday, April 27

Oh, those puppies! The draperies and blankets were blowing on the wash line — a little too close to the ground — and the puppies must have thought, Another New Game! They chased the draperies one way and the draperies chased them back! Then one of the blankets came loose in the wind, and before I could fix it the biggest pup grabbed hold with his teeth and the whole blanket came down on top of him! Off he went — a pink woollen blanket on chubby black legs — with the other pups in pursuit. Mama and I laughed so hard, even though the blanket needed another washing.

Monday, April 30

Hurray! Spring Cleaning is over and Mama has time for more important things — like making Ginger Beer. Now the whole house smells of ginger and lemons and brewer's yeast — a sure sign that summer is on its way — and picnics!

Tuesday, May 1

After school Toby and Andrew and I bottled the Ginger Beer and corked it. Four dozen bottles!

Wednesday, May 2

Heard Sheba growling in the night but paid her no mind, and after a while she stopped. But this morning when I went to collect the eggs I discovered that two of our hens are missing.

Papa came home for a funeral — another railway man was killed by falling rock.

Thursday, May 3

Tonight we shared a bottle of Ginger Beer. Mama declared it fit for use — with just the right amount of sugar — and we heartily agreed. No more tasting, though — we have to wait for the 24th of May. It will be even better by then.

Friday, May 4

A rooster was stolen from Anne's yard.

Saturday, May 5

More missing chickens. Mrs. Murray down the road lost another one. I can't imagine how, with her snarly dogs — unless the thief somehow charmed her dogs the way he must have charmed Sheba. Mrs. Murray says the thief must be caught and given a sound thrashing.

Whoever the thief is, he must be very brave and very hungry.

I wonder why he doesn't ask for food? If he came to our door, Mama would give him something to eat.

Monday, May 14

The puppies are going on 8 weeks old so it is time to give them away. I pleaded with Mama to let me keep little Callie, but Mama was adamant. *All* the puppies must go.

At least Sheba can stay. Mama says she'll make a good watchdog and keep an eye on the Baby. That Baby. I feel very sad. Couldn't Mama let Sheba stay for *me?*

Adamant: firm and unyielding.

Tuesday, May 15

Here is a sketch of Callie.

She looks sad, as if she knows she is going away. I hope her new owner will love her as much as I do.

Wednesday, May 16

The puppies have gone to good homes. One to Constable Lewis, two to friends of Papa's, and Callie has gone to the Schroeders!

Rusty came after school to take her. I picked her up and hugged her, and when she licked my face I started to cry. Rusty made me feel a bit better — he said I could go out to their farm and play with her whenever I liked. And he is not going to change her name.

Saturday, May 19

The chicken thief has been caught. It is a Chinese man who was working for the railway but then the work on his section finished and he and the rest of his gang were told to go. Mama said the poor man is destitute, but the law is the law and his case will go to trial next time Justice Crease comes to town.

Destitute: no money, no food, no place to go. Like the man we found in the snow who lost both his feet. I wonder if he went back to California. Maybe the chicken thief will go back to China. For now he has to stay in jail but at least he is getting food. I asked Mama what they ate in jail but she did not know.

Toby said it would not be chicken because there were no chickens left in town. Mama scolded him for being "insensitive to the plight of others."

Insensitive: lacking feeling.

Plight: bad state or condition.

Sunday, May 20

Four more days until the 24th. The town looks so festive you would think Queen Victoria was coming to *Yale* to celebrate her birthday instead of staying in England. There are flags everywhere, from every single one of her nations. The streets are ready for the races and for once they are free of mud.

Monday, May 21

Today I received a letter from Rachel — written 2 weeks ago — and she is coming to Yale for the 24th. She arrives in 2 days. Her aunt is bringing her up from Victoria and her family is coming down from Spuzzum and they are all staying at the Cascade Hotel. Rachel is allowed to spend one night with me!

Mama said Rachel and her family can join us for our picnic supper. That means feeding twelve people so we will be very busy over the next few days. I do not mind heave-ho-ing when it has to do with picnics.

After school Mama sent me to Mr. Suitto's fruit store for lemons. He has a fresh shipment all the way from California, and they will not last long with the holiday coming up. I bought a whole dozen for a quarter.

Tuesday, May 22

Came home and baked tea cakes and sponge cakes for our picnic. Mama said Anne can come with us, too.

Wednesday, May 23

More delicious chores! Picked rhubarb from the garden, chopped it and stewed it along with dried apples and currants. Then I de-boned the three chickens Mama cooked yesterday. She is going to make a galantine.

Anne came over after supper and we were right in the middle of squeezing lemons when who should walk in but Rachel. We had a grand time talking and laughing and making lemonade. Mama had to tell us to mind what we were doing and not forget the sugar.

Rachel told us all about Angela College and Victoria and how much she liked it and how Yale seemed small and dull by comparison.

After Anne went home, Rachel and I got ready for bed and talked for hours. She said she would be home in July and I could come and spend 2 whole weeks at Aspen Hill Farm. We could even take the horses into the hills and go camping.

Rachel finally talked herself out and fell asleep. But I'm too excited so I'm writing in my Diary. I can't wait until July. I can't wait until tomorrow!

Thursday, May 24

Hip, hip, holiday!

The celebration began at sunrise with a gun salute to honour Queen Victoria — so everyone got off to an early start.

Rachel went to the Cascade Hotel to join her family for breakfast and I spent the morning finishing our picnic preparations. Then I went to Front Street for the Sports. The town was bursting with merry-makers. There were hundreds of railway workers and people from up and down the line, and more "Hip, hip, hurrays!" for Queen Victoria than I could imagine.

The Sports began promptly at 1 oClock with the Indian Canoe Race. One canoe had ten Indians and one had nine, and the smaller canoe won the race. Then there was Hammer Throwing, Shot Putting, Horse Races, a Fireman's Race and Tug-of-War.

Anne and Rachel and I competed in the Sack Race and the Girls' Race. You were supposed to be under twelve, but since there were no races for girls over twelve, we were allowed. Rachel refused to go in the Leapfrog Race or the Three-legged Race. Too unladylike, she said — this, coming from Rachel! — but I did not care, and neither did Anne. We entered the Three-legged Race and *won*!

We watched the Chinese Race and the Indian Race and the Wheelbarrow Race, and cheered for Papa running in the Barrel Race. Poor Papa, he did not come close to winning.

Then there was the Greased Pig Race, with such squealing and shouting and laughing — men and boys tripping and rolling about and the poor pig flinging black mucky grease everywhere. Mama was cross because I got too close and now my frock is splattered with grease, but she could not stay angry because Andrew caught the pig. Lucky us! We'll be having no end of bacon and pork chops.

After the Sports we all rode on a flatcar to Emory Creek for our picnic supper. Mama spread a table-cloth over the grass and we put a stone on each corner to keep it in place. Rachel offered to set the "table," to show what she'd learned at Angela College, but it was no different from what Mama had taught me — knives, forks, spoons, tumblers and plates, all in their proper places.

Then the feast! Out came:
the beefsteak pie
chicken galantine

lettuce torn into pieces and wrapped in a napkin
six small rolls of bread
my tea cakes and sponge cakes and stewed fruit
a pint mould containing apricot cream
3 tiny packets of twisted white paper with salt,
    pepper and sugar
3 small bottles containing salad oil, French
    vinegar and mustard
a white china jar with small balls of butter and
    a tiny branch of parsley
a small tin of thick, sweet cream to pour over
    the stewed fruit.

Goodness knows how we packed so much food into two baskets.

Another hamper contained:
a large jug of cold water
4 bottles of lemonade
4 bottles of lime cordial
6 bottles of ginger beer.

We loaded our plates and merrily tucked in. Then, near disaster! I thought everything tasted just right, but some of our party found the lemonade too sour and the galantine too bland, so they added sugar to the one and salt to the other, following the labels I had written on the twists of paper. But Great Godfrey, I had somehow muddled up the labels, so salt was sugar and sugar was salt. Fortunately the mistake was discovered before too many dishes —

and appetites — were ruined.

We returned to Yale at dusk, well and truly stuffed — and just in time for the dancing. A platform had been put up behind the Palace Hotel, in the middle of the trees, and Chinese lanterns were hanging from the branches. It looked like a fairy land.

I danced the Virginia Reel three times, first with Papa as my partner, then with Rusty, then with Anne. Rachel danced all three reels with Andrew.

Except for the salt and sugar mistake, it was a perfect day.

Private Thought: I liked dancing with Rusty.

Now I am going to bed, although I think I am still too wound-up to sleep.

Friday, May 25

This morning I stopped at the Cascade Hotel to say goodbye to Rachel. We hugged each other and cried and said we couldn't wait until July for our camping trip. Then I went to school and she and her aunt went on the stern-wheeler back to Victoria.

After school, Anne and I walked up the Wagon Road to look for wild strawberries. The Road is finally in good condition — except for the dust — and there is hardly any freighting going on. For once we can go for a stroll and not have to clear the way for ox teams or mule trains, because the railway cars and *Skuzzy* are taking the freight up the line.

But now we have to clear the way for people! Anne wondered why there were so many workers going through Yale and I told her it is because the Upper Section is almost finished. So workers are coming in droves to finish the Lower Section, the part that goes through the Fraser Valley to the Pacific Coast.

Some gangs are going west from Emory to Port Moody and at the same time, other gangs are working east from Port Moody to Emory. Anne said she hopes the two ends meet where they are supposed to! I hope so, too.

While all this is going on, workers are laying track in other Sections, all across the country. Pretty soon — no one knows exactly when — the tracks pushing west from the Rocky Mountains will meet the tracks going east from Savona's Ferry and that will be the end! I mean the end of construction. Because it will also mean the *beginning* of the great Canadian Pacific Railway.

Anne asked if I knew how long the whole railway would be once it was finished and I said close to 3000 miles.

Later I asked Papa how many bridges and trestles there were and he said the Pacific Section alone has 600. But he is not in charge of them all.

Monday, May 28

Cloudy and cool.

Rusty wasn't at school today. Clara told us that some of their cattle wandered onto the track, just below the Powder Works, and a locomotive ran into them. One died and another was injured. So Rusty stayed home to help butcher the dead one.

Thursday, May 31

Melissa was very excited today because her cat, Molly, had kittens and she gets to keep one.

Monday, June 4

Mama feeling poorly. I stayed home from school and washed the linen and now my back and shoulders ache something terrible. Great Godfrey, what a chore! Fill the copper with water and soap. Boil the linen for half an hour. Lift it out and rinse through two clean waters. Hang it out to dry. Pray it does not rain. Or pray it does, for an extra rinse.

Tuesday, June 5

"Played the devil" at the *Sentinel* after school and got my hands and fingers thoroughly inked. Now they are scrubbed to the bone and fair near bleeding. So Mama can stop scolding and I can get down to the important business of writing in my Diary.

Mr. Hagan told me he went to the trial of the chicken thief so he could report it in the *Sentinel*. Here is what happened. Justice Crease passed two sentences. A man who stabbed another man got three years in the penitentiary. The man who stole chickens because he was desperately hungry got four years.

There are so many things I do not understand about the world. For instance, why is a judge called *Justice*? I do not see any justice in these sentences. Especially after I learned that the stabber had been *a soldier* in the *British Service* and served under *Justice Crease's brother*. Does that have anything to do with the sentence? And then there is the fact that the chicken thief is Chinese. Does *that* have anything to do with the sentence?

I discussed this with Anne and she said she thought the sentence was fair because the Chinese man had stolen more than six chickens and inconvenienced a great many people.

Her words made me livid. How could a few missing chickens be compared to a Serious Personal Injury? The stabbed man could have died! He could be maimed for life!

She told me to calm down, that she was only playing "the devil's advocate."

I'd forgotten about "the devil's advocate." We

learned about it last week during a lesson on Debating. It means taking the opposite view from someone for the sake of argument.

Anne said she agreed with me, that the sentence was certainly not fair. We decided that if we were the Justice, we would sentence the Chinese man to one year and the knife-wielding brute to twenty.

I heard there was yet another accident up the line. A man was doing some bridge work and broke his leg.

Papa, please be safe.

Wednesday, June 6

Today Rachel is fourteen. I hope she is having a happy birthday at Angela College. I hope she likes my letter and the handkerchief I sent her. I hope she does not mind that Anne crocheted most of the lace. I hope she writes back soon.

Hope, hopeful, hopeless Kate.

Thursday, June 7

Cold and rainy today. I feel very low.

Only four months until the Baby arrives. I want a sister, but I'm certain that Toby is right.

If it is a girl, Papa will love her best.

Sunday, June 10

Papa went to the Fire Brigade meeting last night. This morning he checked our stovepipes and chimneys and said they were in good order. He told us we have to keep the backyard free from straw or anything else that can be ignited because the dry weather will soon be here and we have to be prepared.

Sometimes I wake up in the night, certain that I can smell smoke or hear the crackle of flames. Then I realize it is my imagination.

I still remember the fire two years ago. It was August 18, 1881. I had gone to Mr. Suitto's for oranges and was walking home along Front Street. One minute it was a hot and dusty summer afternoon, the next minute it was a blazing inferno.

I was directly in front of the Caledonia Hotel when I saw the fire burst out of the roof, right near the chimney, and in seconds the whole roof was a mass of flames. People were yelling from the upper storey, shouts and cries filled the street, the locomotive engine whistled the alarm. Then Kimball and Gladwin's General Store caught on fire, then the building next to it, then the Palace Hotel, all on the north side of the street.

People were rushing everywhere, removing goods from the buildings that were not yet ablaze and piling them up on the south side of the street to be safe, but it was no use. In minutes the flames had spread to the south.

The roof of the Express building was on fire, and Mr. Suitto's fruit store, and the doctor's office and Schroeder's Butcher Shop, and the big brick Oppenheimer building. One store after another went up in flames — the Chemist Shop, Mr. Clair's Bakery and Confectionery, the Post Office, Gilmore and Clark's Dry Goods, Mr. McQuarrie's boot and shoe shop, the California House, saloons, barber shop, coach house, Mr. Tuttle's new restaurant — all this was on Front Street, and on Douglas Street, up behind Front, people's homes were burning, as well as the Jail and Government House.

I wanted to go home but the heat was too intense. So along with everyone else I fled to the east end of town.

When the fire was finally out, we could see that the entire block was destroyed — what everyone called the heart of the town. Everything was gone — except for a few chimneys, part of the stone walls of the Jail, two brick walls of Oppenheimer's store, Mr. Clair's oven and Mr. Tuttle's cottage. It was saved because two brave ladies rushed to the rescue and extinguished the flames.

That part of town was a grim sight for weeks. But people started to rebuild and the clean smell of new wood soon replaced the smell of smoke.

I did not know all the details at the time, being too confused and frightened. Later I learned that there was not enough water pressure to properly fight the fire. And there were not enough men to fight it, as they were too busy saving their own goods.

Last year the Fire Brigade got an engine, a hose cart and a hose. And this summer the water tanks are being repaired. Papa says we are being well looked after. I hope so.

Monday, June 11

Received an invitation to Clara's birthday party on June 25th, a fortnight from now.

She will be eleven years old. I hope it won't rain because we're going to play croquet! I've never played before and I can't wait to try.

Tuesday, June 12

Another railway worker killed today, by falling rock.

Thursday, June 14

Terrible news today. I thought my worst night-mare had come true because the Railway Superintendent told Mama he had received a telegram saying a part of a bridge had collapsed — and it's Papa's bridge! Eight men were killed and ten wounded, including Papa — but thankfully, his injuries are not serious. He is coming home tomorrow.

Friday, June 15

Papa is home. He told us more about the bridge accident. Part of the framework gave way and the men and timbers fell 70 feet. Only one man was killed, not eight, but there were lots of injuries — broken legs and arms and severe concussions. One man is still senseless. Papa says he is lucky he escaped with only a fractured wrist and bruises, but he feels terrible about the other men.

Saturday, June 16

Went up the hill with Anne. Saw a bear and two cubs, but they were a good distance away and paid us no mind.

Got home and made a jam roly-poly to cheer Papa up. He is sad about the accident and feels responsible because he is the Foreman — even though he was not to blame.

Monday, June 18

Plans are afoot. Mama and Papa speak in hushed voices and whenever I'm in earshot — or whenever Toby and Andrew are about — they stop talking altogether. Have they changed their minds about sending me to Angela College? Now I'm not sure if I want to go or not. Rachel still has not answered my last letter.

At school today Rusty told us how he had helped his father put in their croquet court. I wish we could do the same in our yard, but you need a flat lawn. We do not have room for a lawn, flat or otherwise. Too many chickens, vegetable plots, fruit trees and flower beds.

Four more days of school! Next month Rachel will be home. I can't wait to visit her in Spuzzum and go horseback riding. I wonder if Starlight will remember me.

Tuesday, June 19

Went to Gilmore and Clark's with Mama after school to pick out a new hat. Anne was there, too, and we tried on one hat after another until our mothers got annoyed and said, "If you do not make up your minds this instant, we will do it for you." So we each picked a straw boater. Mine has a pink ribbon and Anne's has blue, so we won't get them mixed up when we wear them to school or to Clara's party.

Thursday, June 21

Yesterday it was almost 90 degrees in the shade and today was the same. When there is a breeze it is like a puff from a furnace. The streets are inches deep in dust.

We had our end-of-term concert this afternoon and the school was so crowded with parents it felt even hotter. We sang songs and did recitations, and at the end, Teacher made an announcement — "At a special examination held on May 13, Andrew Cameron passed the standard required for admission to a High School." Andrew bowed and everyone clapped.

We got out of school at 3:30 and the heat was fairly melting.

In the evening I walked up the hill with Anne, thinking it would be cooler, but the mosquitoes were thick as pudding and we failed to find a breath of fresh air. We came back down and Papa built a smudge so we could sit on the verandah.

Now Anne has gone home and my arm is so worn out from flapping at mosquitoes and smudge-smoke I can scarcely hold my pen. Good thing there is nothing more to write about.

Friday, June 22

103 degrees in the sun and 98 degrees in the shade. My brain feels sluggish and sticky, like Syrup of Squill's. At least school is out. I won't have to use my brain until the Fall.

Saturday, June 23

The cat is out of the bag. At dinner tonight Papa announced that Andrew will be going away to Victoria to attend High School. He will board with Mama's cousins who recently arrived from England. Papa will accompany him in August and help him get settled.

All through dinner Andrew looked like the cat that swallowed the canary, and not the least bit surprised. He must have known all along and never breathed a word. Now he speaks of nothing else. His entire future is planned — first, Victoria High School, then on to university to study medicine. In *England*, no less — or so he hopes.

Andrew has clearly been thinking of more than hunting trips. Mama calls him "a dark horse."

Sunday, June 24

Rained all night and into the morning. The rest of the day was blissfully cool and pleasant.

My brothers have switched personalities. Toby scarcely says a word and mopes about with a face as long as a turnip. Andrew talks of nothing but his Glorious Future.

Poor Toby. Is he sad because Andrew is going to Victoria or because *he* has to stay behind in Yale? Either way, he will miss Andrew.

I miss Andrew already and he has not yet gone.

Monday, June 25

I'm home from Clara's party and so full of strawberries and cream I could scarcely touch my dinner. At least, that is the excuse I gave Mama. It is not the whole reason. I feel sick inside because of a terrible row I had with Anne.

We were walking home together, talking about this and that, happy as can be — and suddenly something boiled up and over into a huge great mess of words and feelings.

It started when Anne said, "I'm glad Rachel isn't coming home for the holidays because then you and I can spend more time together."

I said, "What do you mean? Rachel is coming home in July and I'm going to Spuzzum."

"No," she said, "Rachel has changed her mind. She is spending the entire summer with her new friends in Victoria."

Anne's words hurt me to the bone. Was this true? Why had Rachel not told me? And how did Anne come to know of it?

Well, it turns out Rachel's mother was in the Chemist Shop the other day. Anne said hello — she had met her at the May 24th picnic — and asked after Rachel. She told Mrs. Perkins that I was really looking forward to going to their farm in July — she even said she wished that *she* could go, too. The cheek! I'd like to see Anne on a horse — bareback!

Mrs. Perkins then told her she was surprised I hadn't received a letter from Rachel, explaining her change of plans.

By this time I was furious — with Rachel for not telling me, and with Anne, who seemed to *enjoy* telling me. "Why can't you mind your own business?" I said angrily. "Talking behind my back — you interfering QUIDNUNC!"

"That's just like you, Kate!" She flared up, red in the face. "You and your big words that nobody understands! I don't know why I ever wanted to be your friend."

"Well me neither!" I said. "It's a wonder I'm not dead from amnesia, spending time with a milk sop like you."

"Amnesia? A lot you know, you stupid cow! Amnesia is when you lose your memory! You mean ANEMIA!"

We carried on like that, shouting insults in the middle of the Wagon Road, until Anne started to cry and I lost patience. Then it got worse. I called her a crybaby and said she was no fun, not like Rachel — and she said she hoped I had fun playing by myself all summer since Rachel clearly didn't think I was much fun, otherwise she would be here in a minute.

On and on and on. All the grudges and hurts came out. Me being so stubborn with the jade, ignoring her birthday, writing mean things about her in my Diary —

Then, in the middle of all this, a group of Chinese workers came down the road. "There!" Anne shouted. "Go find a Chinaman for a friend! You like them better than anyone, sticking up for them all the time. It's unseemly! And I lied about the chicken thief — he should have been flogged and sentenced to fifty years!"

I can't remember what I said after that. I'm sure it was something mean.

Now I feel sick at heart as well as in my stomach. Anne must have been harbouring those grudges for *months*. I thought we were friends deep down. But I guess it was only on the surface.

I don't know what to do.

Tuesday, June 26

Mrs. Fox stopped by this morning and asked if I would mind her little ones from time to time, since Mr. Fox is away for the summer and she sometimes needs to come into town for groceries. I told her I'd be pleased as punch. I would be anyway, but especially now since I have no friends.

Sunday, July 1

Today is Dominion Day. Canada is 16 years old, the same age as Andrew. We had a picnic at Emory Creek but nothing else happened. It was the same last year, except last year Papa had to work.

Wednesday, July 4

Went to Emory Creek for another picnic, this time for America's birthday, the Fourth of July. I do not know the exact age of America, only that she is older than Canada and even older than Queen Victoria.

Yale looked festive with flags flying everywhere — the Stars and Stripes, the Union Jack and our own Dominion Colours. There was a gun salute at sunrise, like on the 24th of May, and lots of races, but we spent the entire day eating and splashing about at Emory Creek.

Rusty and Clara were there, and Callie too! We were having such fun playing "Fetch" — Callie loves the water! Then Anne came along. She spoke to Rusty and Clara and made a fuss of petting Callie, but she ignored me. And I ignored her.

Other than that I had a grand time. Of course it was nothing like the Fourth of July in 1881. That was really special. People came from everywhere, even as far away as New Westminster and Victoria, to ride on the *first* Excursion Train ever to run upon the Canadian Pacific Railway in British Columbia. I still remember the excitement as we climbed onto the flatcars and took our seats. They were specially built for the occasion and still smelled of new wood. The Conductor shouted "All Aboard," the Brass Band from New Westminster struck up a tune, the whistle blew and the train set off for Emory.

It was a thrilling ride, for the train moved faster than anyone expected, and before long we were in Emory. There was a dancing platform near the American Hotel and some people danced and others went sightseeing. We had our picnic and watched the horse racing and then got on the train to go back to Yale. And lucky us — the Conductor and Engineer had a surprise in store! They took us straight past the town and up through Tunnels 1 and 2!

There was another train, too, and all day long the two trains carried people back and forth from Yale to Emory and from Emory to Yale. The Excursion was to raise money for the benefit of the Yale Fire Brigade, since the disastrous fire of July 1880 (the one we missed) was still fresh in everyone's mind. It was also to celebrate the Fourth of July. So there was no end to the merry-making. Little did we know that another disastrous fire was but 6 weeks away.

I did not have a Diary then, so I'm writing about the Excursion now before I forget everything. And now that I'm done, I am off to bed.

Thursday, July 5

Papa is back at work. I told him to be careful.

Tuesday, July 10

Bush fires burning west of town.

Thursday, July 12

Bush fires burning closer to town. Mama told me not to fret because the Fire Brigade has a new engine and they would soon have the fires under control.

Fretted anyway. And not only about the fires.

Friday the 13th

Called on Anne but Charlotte said she was out. She wasn't — I saw the curtain move in her bedroom window. What did I expect? It is an unlucky day.

Saturday, July 14

Spent the day at the Foxes', minding Melissa and her three little brothers. The boys were as good as gold, especially the baby. Melissa and I played with her kitten, Snowball.

The bush fires are under control. Everyone says the worst is over.

Monday, July 16

Felt miserable and sad the whole livelong day. Even "playing the devil" failed to cheer me up. Mr. Hagan asked why I was so glum and before I knew it, everything came pouring out — Andrew going away, Rachel staying in Victoria, my row with Anne, my not wanting to go to Angela College when I thought I had to, but desperately wanting to once I found out about Rachel, my crochet turning out as badly as my embroidery and knitting and all for the wretched Baby, the railway being almost finished in this Section and then where will we go? I told him

I do not want to move again, not ever, at least not to a place where I'll be a stranger and have to make new friends — but what is the sense of making friends anyway? They are bound to disappoint you. And there is no sense making plans because they never turn out the way you want them to and life is exceedingly unfair.

When I finally stopped for a breath Mr. Hagan told me an ancient Chinese folktale. It goes like this:

Once upon a time a man's horse ran away. His friends said, "How terrible." And the man said, "Maybe."

A few days later his horse returned along with a wild horse that was stronger and healthier. The man's friends said, "How wonderful!" And the man said, "Maybe."

The next day the man's son tried to ride the new horse but he fell off and broke his leg. Everyone said, "How terrible." And the man said, "Maybe."

And then a week later there was a war. All the young men had to go and fight — except for the son with the broken leg. The man's friends all said, "How wonderful! Everything has turned out for the best."

And the man said, "Maybe."

I have thought about this story a fair bit and understand its meaning — although I do not see what it has to do with me. And I do not understand how anyone could accept life's trials as calmly as the man with the horse.

I feel badly about some of the things I said

to Mr. Hagan. Especially when I called the Baby "wretched."

Tuesday, July 17

Andrew and Toby are going camping and said I can go with them. It is not for another week or so, but I'm already excited. Andrew said it would be a Final Adventure for the Knights of the Thistle, before he goes off to High School.

A final Adventure? We never had a *first* Adventure.

Thursday, July 19

It is snowing! Not real snow, but fluffy white cottony snow from the cottonwood tree. The wind is blowing it everywhere.

Saturday, July 21

Papa is home. I was *not* listening at doors but a few moments ago, when I was walking past the parlour, I heard Mama say something about "the last chance" and "the last summer." She sounded sad. Then Papa mentioned the Baby and he sounded so happy I could not bear to hear another word.

Sunday, July 22

Papa has gone off again, but before he left he made two announcements — one good, one bad (maybe).

The good: when Andrew goes to Victoria, Toby and I can go, too!

The maybe bad: when we are in Victoria, Papa is going to meet with a Mr. Dunsmuir who is planning to build a railway on Vancouver Island. The railway will run from Esquimalt to Nanaimo.

Papa would say nothing more about the matter, so my burning questions are unanswered.

Does this mean we will be moving to Vancouver Island? When? Where? To Esquimalt? To Nanaimo? Somewhere in between? Where exactly are those places? What are they like?

Too much to fret about. I am off to bed.

Monday, July 23

A man working above Boston Bar had a narrow escape from a giant powder shot. The shot failed to go off as expected and when the man went back to look, the explosion took place. A big piece of rock struck him on the shoulder. He has a severe wound.

I hope I can sleep tonight without nightmares. God bless Papa and keep him safe from explosions. And collapsing bridges.

Tuesday, July 24

I'm thinking of writing a letter to Anne, apologizing for being peevish, self-centred, big-worded and cruel. I know I have treated her badly — I've been reading my Diary and the proof is in the pages. I've treated her as badly as Rachel treated me when I first came to Yale — except that Rachel threw pine cones instead of words.

I've also been thinking about the first entry I wrote in my Diary. And my LESSON LEARNED: Next time, I will be the *first* to jump out of the boat.

I still feel the same way. But here is the difference — I would not let go of the rope. Rachel blamed the current. I like to think that if my friend were still in the boat, I would *hold fast* and pull her safely to shore.

Could I tell Anne that in a letter?

Wednesday, July 25

I have not yet written to Anne. I saw her in town this morning and she deliberately looked the other way. I never dreamed she could be as stubborn as I am. But Mercy McGinnis, one of us has to make the first move.

Thursday, July 26

I saw Mrs. Perkins in town today and asked about Rachel. She said she was sorry Rachel had not come home for the holidays — she knew I must be disappointed — but her new friends at Angela College, two sisters, had invited her to their home at Shawnigan Lake, near Victoria.

I told her I would be in Victoria around the 13th of August, and she said I could see Rachel at Angela College, because that is the week the girls get settled in for the new term.

Then she told me that I was always welcome to visit Aspen Hill Farm, with or without Rachel. I could even bring my friend Anne and ride the horses.

If only I could!

Saturday, July 28
Morning

Camping! The sky is deep blue and cloudless. My knapsack is packed — except for my Diary — and I am ready to go. Sheba is coming, too.

Evening

We set up our camp in a clearing on the mountain and I am now sitting beside the campfire, pencil in hand and Diary on knee. Sheba is lying beside me. Toby and Andrew are washing our supper dishes in the creek — a detail worth recording — and whistling. I hear rock rabbits whistling, too.

We had wanted to leave at the crack of dawn but by the time we had done our chores and packed everything — food, dishes, blankets and so forth — it was almost noon. Mama told us to enjoy ourselves and watch out for each other. And if we were not home for supper on Tuesday, she would send someone out looking.

We climbed up the mountain trail through dogwood and alder and birch. Saw a fine grey wolf but it quickly disappeared before Andrew could fire. Picked lots of huckleberries and ate them on the way.

At the spot where we cut down our Christmas tree, we stopped and ate some bread and cheese. We had planned to camp there but Andrew suggested we find a spot closer to water. So we kept on going and a short time later found a lovely clearing close to the creek. Thank goodness, as I was getting very hot and tired.

Andrew and Toby put up their tent — I decided to sleep outside — and then we all cut balsam branches to sleep on.

Andrew told us that sleeping on balsam keeps you from catching cold. And balsam contains a resin used in medicine. He told us the name, but I have forgotten.

Andrew amazes me. I used to tease him for thinking he knew everything, and lo and behold, he does! I expected Toby to make some sort of cheeky remark — along the lines of *Doctor* Cameron — but he refrained. (Another detail worth noting.) Perhaps Toby is equally amazed at our Dark-Horse brother.

All that aside, the balsam is very aromatic and soft to lie on. I am sure I'll wake up feeling refreshed and healthy — unless it rains or I'm eaten alive by mosquitoes.

After our "beds" were prepared, Toby started a fire while Andrew mixed flour and water and salt — I labelled the paper twists correctly this time — and made bannock. That was our supper, along with a heated tin of beans and some bacon cooked in the frying pan. I have never tasted anything so delicious. But I expect it was the fresh air and vigorous hike that stimulated my appetite.

Afterwards we drank coffee. Andrew made it too strong but I put in lots of sugar and did not grumble.

I think I might write a story — "The Knights of the Thistle Go Camping" — and enter it in one of the *Girl's Own Paper* competitions. I know they accept entries from Canada. But what if the editors said something cruel? I've read enough of the G.O.P. to know that they always comment on the entries, and often criticize the contributors' handwriting or use of English. No one would know it was me (except me), but imagine reading, "Kate from Canada, your handwriting is shocking!" I would be mortified and hurt to the bone.

Night

The sun has dipped below the mountains.

Andrew has doused the fire and I have thoroughly doused the ashes so we can sleep without fear of setting the woods ablaze.

Toby has devised a light by hammering three nails into a piece of wood into the ground, and setting a candle inside. Now that I can see to write, I think I'll write a poem.

The mountains look ghostlike
With the moon silvering their tops
Not a breath of air
Nor stirring breezes –

Later

Bannock and bullocks! It is hard to write a poem. I am far too weary to think or write. So I'm off to my balsam-branch bed.

My first night sleeping under a canopy of stars! And a whole day not thinking about Anne. Until now.

Sunday morning, July 29

Woke to a chorus of birds after an exceedingly restless night. Snorts, hoots, sniffs, an occasional howl, the endless whine of mosquitoes — it seemed as if a whole mountain of wildlife was out and about exploring our campsite. With Sheba's growling and barking and scratching it is a wonder I slept a wink.

Got up, picked balsam needles out of my hair (my hair smells aromatic but a little too much like Turpentine), then splashed creek water over my face.

I am presently sitting beside a stone-cold camp-fire, wondering what to do. No sign of Sheba or my brothers. I did not hear them get up and do not know where they have gone — hunting, I suppose, because they have taken their rifles. Why did they go without waking me? When will they be back?

I could start a fire. Boil water. Cook breakfast. I should make lots of noise so the bears will keep their distance.

I feel lonely and tired and wish I were home. The minute I get home I am going to swallow my pig-headedness, write a letter to Anne and deliver it to her in person.

Sunday morning, a few moments later

Went to the creek for some water and saw smoke rising above the trees. Smelled it, too. Still a good ways off but the wind is blowing in this direction and I'm frightened. Called Sheba and my brothers — no answer — must not panic.

Sunday evening, July 29

I'm home.

I have a burn on my hand — my left hand, so I can still write — my knees are scraped, my arms are scratched, my hair is singed, the clothes I was wearing — shoes, stockings, pinafore — are black with soot and fairly ripped to shreds. My new straw boater with the pink ribbon is nowhere to be found. I expect it is burnt to ashes.

In spite of Mama's ointments and syrups I ache all over, inside and out, from tip to toe. I am also exhausted. Too exhausted to write another word.

Monday, July 30, 10 A.M.

It rained overnight and the wind changed direction so the fire has been checked. There is no danger to the town, but sparks were thrown into the bush on the opposite side of the river and that caused a forest fire that is burning yet.

Mama told me I slept for over 12 hours. I am feeling much better — except for some stiffness and a few aches and pains — so here is the rest of my account. I can't call this part "The Knights" etc. because there was only me.

The moment I decided to leave our camp, I put my Diary in my knapsack and started down the trail. I kept yelling for Toby and Andrew and Sheba but there was still no answer so I gave up when my voice gave out.

By this time it seemed like the whole mountainside was on fire. Smoke, wind, flames, trees burning and crackling and falling with a crash — I followed the trail and came round a bend and horrors! — the trail was blocked by a fallen tree, branches aflame and higher than my head. A spark blew into my hair, got caught in my plait — I smelled it burning — brushed it away, burned my hand and singed my hair. I ran to the creek a little ways to the right, plunged in and soaked myself, head to toe, splashed water on my knapsack and carried on. I could scarcely breathe for fear, but knew that if I followed the creek I would get to the river and home.

I stumbled over rocks and through brambles, barely able to see — eyes stinging, lungs bursting, clothing scorched and torn, the wind carrying sparks and new fires flaring up everywhere. Finally came in sight of the river and the Wagon Road —

saw the Powder Works and Mr. Onderdonk's place and people carrying furniture out of his house — saw the railway bridge in flames, west of the Powder Works, and people trying to put out the fire by hand. Two Wagon Road bridges further to the west were also burning.

I saw ladies, children and a few men hurrying along the road toward town and I had almost caught up to them when a tremendous explosion knocked me off my feet. The Powder Works! The ground shook like an earthquake and I felt the whole world was about to end. When the shaking stopped I got up and saw the Powder Works blazing, and beside it the Fox house, and down the road Mrs. Fox and her baby and two little boys, but no Melissa. I called out, "Where's Melissa?" and Mrs. Fox looked around, confused, and said, "She was right here," then, "Dear God, she's gone back for her kitten!"

All this happened faster than it takes to tell, let alone to write. Mrs. Fox had no sooner spoken than we both saw the fire spread to the house with Melissa most likely inside. I ran as fast as I could and pushed open the door, screaming for Melissa — and found her trying to coax the kitten out from under her bed. By this time the heat was intense and the roof was on fire and the smoke near suffocating. I grabbed Melissa and ran back outside as the entire west side of the house went up in flames. The whole time, Melissa clung to me and cried for her kitten and all I could do was cry too.

Then a second, more powerful explosion erupted from the Powder Works. Everyone fell to the ground, Melissa clutching me in terror and me pretending to be brave and telling her she was safe — and poor Mrs. Redgraves who lives next door to the Nitro-glycerine House, near the bank of the river — the force of the explosion threw her right out of a window and into the road. Mr. R. went to her aid and she was able to get to a place of safety.

Through all this — smoke, flames, explosions, people rushing about and cursing the New Engine (which reached the Powder Works too late to do any good) — somehow in all the confusion and panic I made my way home.

Melissa came with me — she would not let go of my hand — and her mother and brothers came, too. Mama said they could stay with us until they got their bearings and Mrs. Fox said thank you, and accepted Mama's offer — but only until Tuesday when she will go to Hope and meet up with her husband.

Mama gave everyone some supper — I could not manage a bite — and arranged for beds and blankets. Melissa slept with me and is sleeping yet.

As soon as I finish this account, I'll look for some of my outgrown pinafores for Melissa. Mama was saving them to cut down for the Baby but poor Melissa lost everything in the fire and Mama won't mind.

Monday afternoon

My brothers told me that on the morning of our camping trip they got up early to go hunting, and since I was sound asleep they did not want to disturb me. They went farther than they should have gone but hurried back as soon as they saw the smoke. Then they discovered I had already left. They packed up hastily and circled off to the east instead of going down the trail, because of the way the wind was blowing. They said they were sorry, they should never have gone off and left me, they thought at first I had gone home long before the fire, then they were afraid I was dead, especially when they heard the explosion. They said the same things so many times I finally told them to be quiet. I'm not dead, but *they* might be if they do not give me some peace.

I cannot be too cross with them because they found my straw boater at the campsite and brought it home.

Now I have a thought. Maybe Mr. Hagan will publish my account in the *Sentinel*. AN ARDUOUS ADVENTURE by Kate Cameron. Or

Kathleen L. Cameron? K.L. Cameron? I can't decide.

Mama told me that Anne came over while I was asleep and brought me some sweet peas from their garden. They smell like summer.

LESSON LEARNED: Sometimes your worst fears come to life and there is nothing to do but face them head on as best you can. Everyone says I was brave and clear-headed and a real little heroine to go into the house for Melissa. I did not feel brave. I felt sick with fear from the moment I first saw the smoke and started down the trail. As for Melissa, I did not stop to think, I just rushed in, faster than anyone else. I might have been more foolish than clear-headed.

I wish I could have saved her kitten. A horse was killed, too. It was tied up near the west end of the Powder Works.

The Foxes' cat, Molly, was safe. Someone found her on the river bank.

Now I'm going to leave off writing and have something to eat. Then I'll go to the Church and help Mama and the ladies. They are collecting and sorting donations for the Foxes — and for the Olsons, who also lost their home and belongings in the fire.

And tomorrow I will call on Anne.

Melissa and her mother and brothers left this morning. The house is very quiet and I am very weary.

Last night, Melissa had a nightmare and woke up crying. She kept thinking about her kitten and was afraid our house would catch fire or explode. I told her she was safe, it was raining, the fires would be out, there was no dynamite left to explode — I tried everything to calm her but nothing worked. I was getting so desperate I was about to wake her mother, but I suddenly remembered "The Song of the Locomotive." I recited it several times, with dramatic flair (I thought) and perfect enunciation, but then I had to do it in a whisper because Toby banged on the wall and told me to hush.

Melissa told me her favorite line — "I roar on the beach of the roaring deep" — so I made up a new poem that goes like this:

I roar on the beach of the roaring deep
And put Melissa and Kate to sleep.

She liked that very much and said it over and over until it worked.

We got up early (in spite of being awake half the night) and had oatmeal porridge and cream for breakfast. It was still raining and the air was black with smoke.

By 8 oClock the Foxes were ready to go. Mama gave Mrs. Fox two big boxes of clothing and linen and cooking utensils — with more to come. I gave Melissa a big hug and promised her one of Sheba's puppies the next time she has a litter.

I walked with them to the steamboat landing. Everyone in town was sweeping up glass from broken windows. Our house had two windows blown out, one in the dining room and one in the parlour. Toby and Andrew swept up the glass yesterday morning while I was asleep.

On the way to the landing, Melissa wanted to hear "The Song of the Locomotive" a few more times and now she knows it almost by heart. I think it helped take her mind off things.

They left on the stern-wheeler and I went to see Anne. She was in her father's shop, sweeping up glass from broken bottles and windows. I thanked her for the flowers and told her I was sorry. She said she was sorry, too.

Then I gave her one half of the jade that Toby had polished. I said she could either keep it or send it to Princess Louise.

She said she would keep her half as long as I kept mine, and that way we would always be friends. Then we hugged each other and finished sweeping up the broken glass.

Before I left she told me she had no idea jade was so beautiful, once it was cut and polished.

Wednesday, August 1

The entire town is talking about the explosions. Someone said there were 360 cases of Giant Powder stored in the Powder Magazine, equal to 9 tons. It all burned gradually for a time until it caused the second explosion. The first explosion was caused by nitro-glycerine.

Mama says she has always been fearful of a terrible accident. And if Mr. Onderdonk builds another Powder Works, it had better be in a remote location.

Thursday, August 2

The salmon are running and the Indians are on the river with their nets. The sky is hazy but not black. The air does not reek of smoke. I am thankful for a calm and uneventful day.

Wednesday, August 8

Anne and I have spent a wonderful week playing games and visiting friends and strolling up the river. Sometimes we take our sketchbooks and draw pictures to keep as souvenirs.

Sometimes we talk about going back to school on

September 3, with the same old teacher. We call him Mr. Eyebrow (but just between ourselves).

Anne said she is happy I'm not going to Angela College. I am, too. But I feel a little twinge — afraid that we might have to move away from Yale and that is why Papa is going to see Mr. Dunsmuir in Victoria.

Today I went to Anne's for tea and her mother told me I had done Anne the world of good, getting her out and about in the fresh air. "A thin little girl is a pitiable sight," she said, "but look at Anne now. Plump and rosy cheeks, no sign of anemia — the picture of good health — just like you." Hearing this made me blush as much as Anne.

Saturday, August 11

I'm sitting on the steamer on my way to Victoria. It is a fine day, not a cloud in sight. Scenery grand as usual.

Toby and Andrew are strolling around the deck. Papa is sitting beside me reading the paper and smoking his pipe. Mama is only two months away from her confinement so she is staying at home to rest.

We boarded the *Western Slope* early this morning along with a number of other passengers and some freight. The river is low, and every so often the captain slows down the engines to take soundings. When we get to New Westminster we are getting off and spending the night in the Occidental Hotel. I call it the "toothache hotel" because of my last visit, but this time staying there will be a painless treat.

Sunday, August 12

Occidental Hotel, New Westminster, British Columbia

Here I am in our hotel room at the end of a long and pleasant day. Papa wanted to see the terminus of the Canadian Pacific Railway so this morning we got on a stage for Port Moody — and 6 miles of rough-and-tumble over the Wagon Road. The driver stopped his team at the bottom of a long hill and there we were at Port Moody Harbour.

We got out and looked across the water. About 12 miles to the west is what Papa calls Burrard Inlet. One mile to the east is the Government Dock. That is where they are going to build the station. And that is where the railway will end after coming all the way across Canada. Toby said, "No, that's where the railway will BEGIN."

Of course it depends on whichever way you are going.

Papa hired a ferryman and we went across to the Dock. There was a fine three-masted ship from

London, unloading steel rails for the railway. And some buildings that Papa took an interest in, hotels, Government buildings and the like. I became bored and wandered around. Nothing much to write about. Steep hill, swampy ground. *Huge* timber — where it has not been cut down for the railway. Some of the tree trunks look to be 9 feet in diameter.

Papa says there will be a town there one day, even a city, but I find that hard to imagine.

The tide was out so Toby and Andrew walked along the beach and looked for clams and crabs and shells. The smell of low tide makes me feel seasick.

We had lunch in the Caledonia Hotel. Toby told us that he had discovered a trail near the Dock, and by following the trail back to New Westminster instead of taking the ferry and stage, Papa would save $6.00. We took the ferry and stage anyway. It took 2 hours over the bumpy road, even with a four-horse team and a crack-whip driver. Toby said it would have been quicker on the trail as well as cheaper.

Now we are back in the Occidental for the night. It is a grand hotel with forty rooms. Our room is spacious and clean and my bed is very soft.

Tomorrow we go to Victoria and on Monday I'll see Rachel at Angela College. I have not seen her since May and she has not written to me since early

June. I answered her letter then, and asked a number of questions, but she has not yet replied.

There is so much I want to know. Does she sometimes feel sad for no reason? And, a moment later, feel as though her heart might burst with joy? I am on a constant seesaw. Up and down, up and down. Never mind *brothers* driving me to distraction. I can do it well enough on my own.

Monday, August 13

Victoria

I'm writing this at Cousin Lucy's house. It is a grand house on an Inland Waterway called the Gorge. After we got here, Papa hired a hack and we went to Victoria High School so Andrew could register.

Tuesday, August 14

Is there ever an end to Disappointments?

I'm sitting in the swing on Cousin Lucy's verandah, watching the evening sun polish up the Gorge and wondering how someone you think you know can turn out to be so different.

After lunch today, Andrew and Toby went rowing on the Gorge with Cousin Dick, Papa went to see Mr. Dunsmuir, and I finally got to Angela College to see Rachel. She showed me her room and gave me a tour around the school. It is a splendid building with a high board fence. She introduced me to some of the boarders, the ones back from holidays, including the Shawnigan Lake sisters. Most were older than her, she said, but they were a sweet lot of girls and very friendly.

That may have been true for Rachel, but they did not treat me very kindly. I was invited to join them for tea and found it a great strain. I suddenly found myself tongue-tied and awkward, unable to put two words together without stumbling — not that I was given much opportunity to speak, for after a few comments and questions tossed in my direction, Rachel and her friends went on to topics of greater interest — for example, the upcoming Balls at Government House and the handsome Middies from the British Men-of-war at Esquimalt who would attend. They could have been talking Greek for all I understood. At one point I asked, What is a Middie? and they laughed. After that I asked no further questions.

I'm hurt over the way Rachel ignored me at tea, the way she left me sitting there like a lump on a log. Worse, she told her friends about my letter, the one where I asked how she felt about growing up, and where I said that I wished I could have stayed twelve years old forever. They laughed some more and Rachel said she cannot wait to be grown up with hundreds of beaux fighting over her hand.

I felt like saying, "Smarty boots, proudy hoops," like Rachel did when I first arrived in Yale. But I bit my tongue and forced myself to think *Thick Skin*.

Thank goodness I'm not going to Angela College. I would have to leave the real Kate outside the board fence. And if she wandered off, I would be left with a Self I did not know. I think that would be the height of loneliness.

Now I keep wondering about Papa's meeting with Mr. Dunsmuir. Maybe he has signed a new contract and we are about to move again. Maybe not. I am afraid to ask.

Later

I was unable to sleep so I got up, found Papa smoking his pipe on the verandah and asked him straight out if we had to move to Vancouver Island because of Mr. Dunsmuir's Railway. He said, maybe one day, but not for a while.

And then he told me why — in great detail. I did not need such a detailed explanation but once I had the answer to my question I thought it only polite to listen to Papa. And now that I know the reason, and still cannot sleep, I may as well write it down.

There is a bridge being built where the railway

crosses the Fraser River — an Iron and Steel Cantilever Bridge — the first of its kind ever to be built
in North America. Papa is very excited about this
bridge and has signed a contract with Mr. Onderdonk to see it through. It is very complicated. The
bridge is going to be built at Cisco Flat, a little ways
south of Lytton. Sections of the bridge are presently being made in Great Britain and they will be
shipped to Port Moody sometime this year. Papa
says he hopes the railway from Port Moody to Yale
will be finished by the time the sections arrive so
they can get them to the site without any trouble.
Then they will put the bridge across the river. It will
be 142 feet above the water!

I feel very happy. When Papa said we do not have
to move to Vancouver Island I said, "That's wonderful!"

If he was like the man with the horse he would
have said, "Maybe." Instead, he kissed me good night
and said, "I think so, too."

I can't wait to tell Anne.

Now I can go to sleep.

Except for one more thing. I found out that a
Middie is a midshipman — a sailor training to be an
Officer in the Navy. Well, Rachel is welcome to her
Middies. I hope she fares well on rough seas.

Wednesday, August 15

New Westminster

Here I am back at the Occidental. Got up early this A.M. and said goodbye to Andrew and Cousin Lucy. Cousin Dick drove us to the Hudson Bay Company's wharf and we boarded the HBC steamer for New Westminster. Spent almost the entire voyage out on deck and got to N.W. about 3 P.M.

Went for a stroll in the evening and picked some Spirea for Mama. She loves the pink flowers in her flower arrangements.

Toby asked Papa how long it will be before the Pacific Section of the Railway is finished. Papa said the progress of the line between Emory and Port Moody is very rapid. He is certain that the "iron horse" that whistles in Port Moody come Christmas morning will do the same thing in Yale in the evening.

I wonder where I'll be on Christmas morning. I hope I'm home in Yale, sitting by the fire, holding my new sister or brother. I've been thinking about the Baby and have decided that I won't mind so terribly if it is a boy. Goodness, by the time he grows up to be as annoying as Toby, I'll be off in some far-flung corner of the Empire — like Calcutta! — reporting the news of the world.

And if the Baby is a girl? I admit I might be jealous. But only for a little while.

Thursday, August 16

Fraser River

It is 7 A.M. and the steamboat has just left the New Westminster landing. My ears are still ringing from the whistle.

The boat is crowded with people, most of whom I know. Not like my journey three years ago, when I felt strange and out of place and the railway scarcely begun. Sometimes I feel as if the railway and I are growing up together. I do not expect I'll be "finished" at the same time, but to hear Papa talk, the railway may *never* be finished. There will always be something to rebuild and repair and replace — even when the trains are running from sea to sea.

Later

Papa just handed me a package. I opened it and lo and behold — it is a brand new Diary!

Papa said, "I see you've almost finished your first one." This is true — I have but one remaining page — and he told me how pleased he was that I had put it to such good use. He gave me a hug and told me that I would always be his special girl, and that the new Baby will be lucky indeed to have a sister like me to look up to.

I am so anxious to begin my new Diary! Eyes and ears open, thoughts tumbling helter-skelter, emotions about to burst. What lies around the bend? Maybe something Adventurous. Maybe something Exceedingly Wonderful.

It is a beautiful morning. I feel so light of heart I could float up the Canyon, all the way home. And with that happy thought, I come to the end of the very last page.

Epilogue

The Canadian Pacific Railway was completed in November, 1885. A short time later, the Camerons, including Kate's two-year-old sister, Mary, left Yale and moved to Victoria, where John Cameron started working for the Esquimalt and Nanaimo Railway. In 1905, the E & N became part of the CPR.

Michael Hagan stopped publishing the *Inland Sentinel* in Yale on May 29, 1884, but started again in Kamloops, B.C., two months later.

Kate graduated from Victoria High School in 1888 and promptly applied for a job with Victoria's *Colonist*. She was hired as a junior reporter — much to the chagrin of her mother, who saw it as a low-class occupation and not suitable for young ladies.

But times were changing. The career of journalism was opening up to women and, over the next decade, the once low-class occupation became a glamorous pursuit. Kate wrote for several top newspapers, including Toronto's *Globe*. When the *Globe* sent her to the Yukon in 1898 to write about the

Klondike Gold Rush, she met the English photographer Peter Mortimer.

Toby left school and worked for the CPR — first as a wiper, then as a fireman and finally as an engineer, based in Winnipeg. He married and had four children.

Andrew attended university in Toronto and became a doctor. He practised in Northern Ontario for many years and eventually settled in Ottawa with his wife and three children.

Kate married Peter Mortimer in 1900. An adventurous and resourceful team, they travelled the world recording events and experiences through words and pictures. "A letter from Auntie Kate!" was an enthusiastic cry often heard in the homes of her nieces and nephews.

Kate and Peter lived in London, England, from 1908 until war broke out in 1914. Kate then returned to Canada with their two young sons while Peter stayed in Europe to cover the First World War. They were reunited in Vancouver shortly after Armistice Day in 1918.

In spite of her best intentions, Kate eventually lost touch with her friends from Yale. She and her brothers and sister, however, remained close throughout their lives.

Yale's position as a bustling and prosperous town changed once the railway was completed. The transport of freight no longer depended on the steamboats, and the Cariboo Wagon Road, maintained by Onderdonk throughout the construction period, was rendered obsolete. Many families and long-standing businesses moved away. Yale became a station on the main line, where trains stopped but briefly.

The town is still on the map, however, as the gateway to the Fraser Canyon and its rich and fascinating history. Its residents can still hear the rumble of trains as they roll along the tracks.

Historical Note

❧

One country from East to West and a railway to tie it together! Such was the dream of Sir John A. Macdonald, Canada's first Prime Minister. And there was good reason for it. At the time of Confederation, when the colonies of New Brunswick, Nova Scotia, Ontario and Quebec joined together to form the Dominion of Canada, the threat of United States expansion into Canada's largely unsettled north and west was real and imminent. What better way to solve the problem than by building a transcontinental railway? At the same time, it would build up the country from coast to coast and fill the land with settlers who wanted to be Canadians.

To fulfill his dream, Macdonald needed British Columbia. He promised that if B.C. joined Confederation, he would build the railway straight to the shores of the Pacific. In 1871, four years after Confederation, B.C. became the westernmost province of Canada, and Macdonald's dream of an east–west link came one step closer to reality.

Before any tracks could be laid, the land had to be surveyed. Survey crews spent several years struggling through the rock and muskeg of northern Ontario, across the prairie and through the rugged mountains of B.C., looking for the safest, cheapest and most direct route for the railway. Some 19,000 kilometres of wilderness were covered before a final route was determined.

Once the route was mapped out, construction could begin. Roadbeds were cleared, bridges built, tunnels blasted through rock. Tracks were laid and iron spikes hammered to hold the rails in place. Crews worked simultaneously from the east and the west to speed up the process.

The cost of building a transcontinental railway across Canada's vast landscape of mountains, prairies, rivers and swamps was tremendous. For almost two years Macdonald tried to get private funding. Finally, in February, 1881, he secured the backing of a private company — the Canadian Pacific Railway Company. The CPR signed a contract agreeing not only to construct, complete and equip the railway, but also to maintain it and run it forever. In return, the Dominion of Canada agreed to provide the CPR with 25 million acres of land and to pay the company $25 million in cash.

By this time, private contractors hired by the government were already building sections of the railway in central Canada, the eastern prairies and British Columbia. Under the terms of the contract, these sections were also turned over to the CPR once the construction was completed.

Andrew Onderdonk, an American, was the contractor responsible for the Pacific Section — from Port Moody on the coast, through the Fraser Canyon, to Savona's Ferry at the west end of Kamloops Lake. He established his headquarters in Yale in 1879, and on May 15, 1880, a blast of dynamite at Yale marked the start of construction.

The Pacific Section proved to be one of the most remarkable engineering feats in Canada's history. Much of the road had to be suspended over the Fraser River on piles, wooden bridges and rock cribbing. Blasting was necessary to widen the flat surface ledges in the walls of the Fraser Canyon and to tunnel through the granite cliffs. A whole year was spent blasting the right-of-way before any track could be laid.

Then there was the problem of labour. Onderdonk needed as many as 10,000 labourers to build the Fraser Canyon section of the railway, and since B.C.'s labour force at the time was too small to fill the need, he was forced to look elsewhere. In spite of widespread opposition, he arranged for thousands of Chinese labourers to come to British Columbia, most directly from China.

Pushing the line through the Fraser Canyon proved to be costly. One of Onderdonk's contracts alone, the 45-kilometre section between Emory and

Boston Bar (including excavation, grading, tunnelling, bridging, tracklaying and ballasting) cost $2,727,300 (more than 45 million in today's dollars). The estimated cost of the entire Canadian Pacific Railway in 1886 dollars was almost $165 million, including branch lines and existing ones that were acquired, plus those constructed by the government itself.

The high number of accidental deaths and injuries among the workers, as well as the hundreds of deaths caused by scurvy, also made it costly in human terms.

Onderdonk's contract eventually extended from Savona's Ferry, through Kamloops and on to Eagle Pass. Work progressed rapidly until the summer of 1885, when Onderdonk ran out of rails along the Eagle River and dismissed most of his crews.

A few months later, on a cold November day in the British Columbia mountains, crews working from the east linked their rails to those laid by Onderdonk's crews. The site was christened Craigellachie — the name of a rallying-point in Scotland meaning "Rock of Alarm." CPR officials George Stephen and Donald Smith — cousins from Scotland — used the word between themselves during the building of the railway, when times were especially difficult.

The "Last Spike Ceremony" on November 7,

1885, was noted for its simplicity. William Cornelius Van Horne, the CPR's General Manager, had said that there would be no ceremony, at least not an official one. No dignitaries were invited. Anyone who wanted to attend had to be a railway employee or pay their own fare. After Donald Smith hammered in the second 5-inch iron spike — he bent the first one —Van Horne was called upon to make a speech. Not a man to waste words, he simply said, "All I can say is that the work has been well done in every way."

Seven months later, on June 28, 1886, the first passenger train, the Pacific Express, left Montreal for the Pacific Coast. The 150 passengers lucky enough to be on board were entertained by local bands, fireworks and bonfires as the train passed through towns along the way. Travelling at an average speed of 33 kilometres per hour, it covered the distance of some 4700 kilometres in 5 days and 19 hours — and reached Port Moody on time, sharp at 12:00 noon. As one passenger remarked, "A pretty good showing."

Port Moody's role as the Pacific terminus of the transcontinental railway was short-lived. A 12-mile extension to the line, completed in May, 1887, gave that distinction to a new city — a "promising plucky little metropolis" known as Vancouver.

With the completion of the railway came the

opening of the west. Attracted by advertisements calling the vast prairies "the last best west," and by the government's promise of cheap land, thousands of immigrants from Britain, Europe and elsewhere streamed into Canada. Many went west to find farmland or to raise cattle. Others sought employment in the forests and fisheries of B.C.

Trains continually crossed the country, carrying passengers and freight, bringing people to the land and taking raw materials and manufactured items to faraway customers. With trains to carry mail, and the telegraph system built alongside the railway, people were able to communicate as never before. Trade flourished. New wealth poured in. Towns grew up around railway stations. Major cities were founded, including Sudbury, Regina, Calgary and Vancouver.

Thousands of men laboured to build the Canadian Pacific Railway, from Canadians, Americans and British to Germans, Italians and Chinese. Their work, "well done in every way," saw the realization of a dream that not only played a major role in building a strong Canada in the early years of Confederation, but also helped shape the nation into what it is today.

A poster advertising the Canadian Pacific Railway as the primary connection between eastern and western Canada.

The high walls of the Fraser Canyon, showing the Cariboo Wagon Road (at lower right) and the town of Yale in the distance.

The town of Yale, B.C., about 1886.

The schoolhouse in Yale looked very much like this school/town hall in Richmond, B.C., built in 1880.

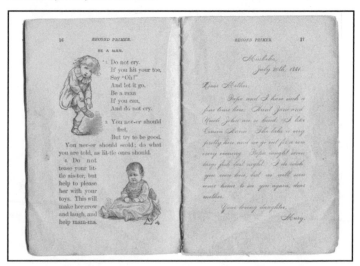

Pages from a primer. Primers were used by young students who were just beginning to read.

Preparation of the roadbed before track is laid. This location is at Sailor Bar Bluff, about 12 kilometres above Yale.

Workers blasting a path through the mountains. This painting of an explosion is by noted Canadian artist C. W. Jefferys.

This 1886 photograph shows an empty ballast train crossing the cantilever bridge spanning the Fraser River at Cisco Flat, 220 kilometres east of Port Moody.

A Chinese work crew during construction of the CPR. Because of the many deaths and injuries to these workers, some Chinese called Hell's Gate "The Slaughter Pen."

Donald Smith, a prominent CPR official, driving the last spike in Craigellachie, B.C. This joined the tracks coming from the east to those built by Andrew Onderdonk's crews, and completed the 4700-kilometre-long Canadian Pacific Railway.

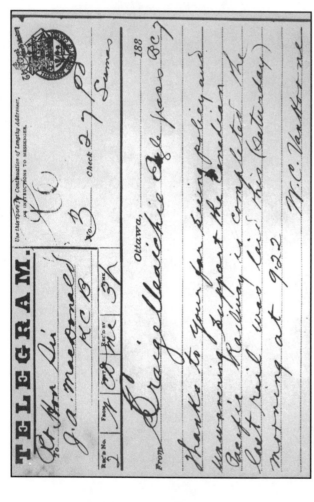

A telegram sent by W.C. Van Horne, the CPR's General Manager, from Craigellachie, B.C., to Prime Minister Sir John A. Macdonald, stating that the tracks for the Canadian Pacific Railway have been completed. (Note Van Horne's unusual spelling: Craigelleaichie.)

The arrival of the first train at Port Moody, at noon on July 4, 1886.

Two transcontinental trains, the Pacific Express *and the* Atlantic Express, *meeting at Rogers Pass. The* Pacific *will reach Port Moody in less than a day. The* Atlantic *will reach Montreal in 4 days. By noted Canadian painter of historic steam locomotives, Wentworth Folkins.*

Prime Minister Sir John A. Macdonald and Lady Agnes Macdonald (standing at upper left), on their way west to the Pacific after the completion of the CPR.

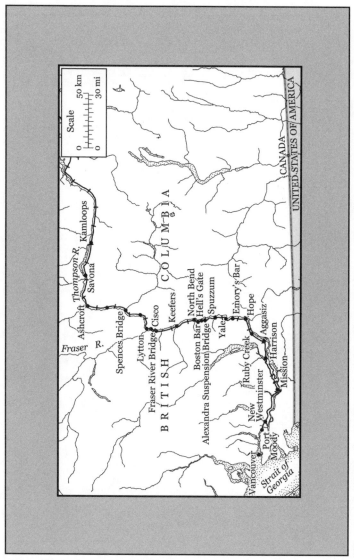

The section of track through the Fraser Canyon, and especially Hell's Gate, was one of the most difficult the railway crews had to complete.

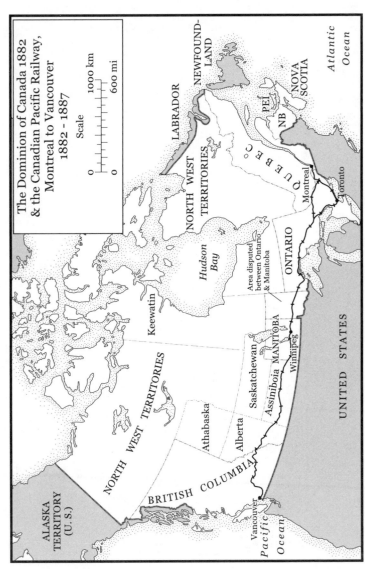

The Canadian Pacific Railway stretching from sea to sea — from Vancouver on Canada's west coast, to the
St. Lawrence River in the east. Tracks also ran farther east to the Atlantic.

Acknowledgments

Grateful acknowledgment is made for permission to reprint the following:

Cover portrait: John Everett Millais, *Bright Eyes* (detail), 1877, Aberdeen Art Gallery and Museums.

Cover background: Wentworth Folkins, *The Transcontinentals Meet at Rogers Pass* (detail), courtesy of Heritage Art Editions Inc.

Page 186: Canadian Pacific Archives, A.6408.

Page 187 (upper): Canadian Pacific Archives, A.11519.

Page 187 (lower): Canadian Pacific Archives, A.11625.

Page 188 (upper): City of Vancouver Archives, OUT P254 N100.

Page 188 (lower): from *Canadian Readers Primer 2*, published by Gage Education; image courtesy of the Royal British Columbia Museum, Victoria, British Columbia.

Page 189 (upper): Canadian Pacific Archives, ns25761.

Page 189 (lower): C. W. Jefferys, *Railway Building / The Pathmakers*, 1912, University of Lethbridge Art Collections. Reproduced with permission of the C.W. Jefferys Estate Archive.

Page 190: Canadian Pacific Archives, A.11416.

Page 191: B.C. Archives, D-07548.

Page 192: Canadian Pacific Archives, NS. 1960.

Page 193: Canadian Pacific Archives, A.93.

Page 194: Canadian Pacific Archives, ns. 19991.

Page 195: Wentworth Folkins, *The Transcontinentals Meet at Rogers Pass*, courtesy of Heritage Art Editions Inc.

Page 196: Canadian Pacific Archives, NS. 10217.

Pages 197 and 198: Maps by Paul Heersink/Paperglyphs. Map data © 2000 Government of Canada with permission from Natural Resources Canada.

Thanks to Barbara Hehner for her careful checking of the manuscript, and to Robert Turner, author of *West of the Great Divide*, for sharing both his historical expertise and his own fascination with trains.

In memory of my parents,
Jean and Charles Goodwin,
and my CPR grandparents,
John and Lydia Anderson —
for all my early journeys on the railway.

An enormous thank you to:
Bruce Mason and Susan Baerg of the Yale and District
Historical Society; P.C. Townsend, who allowed the Yale
reminiscences of his relative, Elizabeth Tatlow, to be
forwarded to me; Stephen Lyons of Canadian Pacific
Archives; the staff at British Columbia Provincial
Archives; Lorne Hammond, Curator in History at the
Royal B.C. Museum; Shirley Cuthbertson, Curator
in History (Retired) at the Royal B.C. Museum;
and my husband, Patrick, whose encouragement
kept me on track right through
to the figurative "last spike."

Other sources that proved invaluable:
Henry and Self *and* By Snowshoe, Buckboard
and Steamer, *books by Kathryn Bridge that include*
the accounts of young women living or travelling
in the Fraser Canyon area in the 1880s;
Onderdonk's Way, *a website that focusses*
on the building of the CPR in the Fraser Canyon;
Michael Hagan's newspaper, The Inland Sentinel,
for information on the progress of the railway,
day-to-day events and weather reports for the period
covered by Kate's diary.

About the Author

∽∘∾

Julie Lawson has travelled by train all through the area where Kate's story is set, "many times — and always in awe. What an extraordinary accomplishment, to build that railway." Her husband, Patrick, is a railway enthusiast who publishes articles and drawings (plans for locomotives, cars, stations, bridges) in model railroad magazines. Julie says she has spent many holidays "alongside the CPR tracks in the Fraser Canyon, waiting for trains to appear, for those perfect photo opportunities." In fact, until recently, her "entire basement was taken up by an enormous HO scale model layout of the Fraser Canyon, all constructed by Patrick. Miles of track, trains, tunnels, bridges, forests, cliffs and river — it was all there, even the maintenance crews. If it had been a historical layout rather than a contemporary one," she adds, "Kate would have been there, too."

Julie's own grandfather, John Anderson, was among the many immigrants needed to keep the CPR running smoothly. He left Sweden in 1888 at the age of eighteen and started working for the railway in the Selkirk Mountains of B.C. By the early 1900s he had married a young Swedish immigrant and advanced to the position of Roadmaster, responsible for the section of track going through Rogers Pass — an area noted for its heavy snowfalls and avalanches.

One of those avalanches almost took his life. "On the night of March 4, 1910, a huge avalanche came down at the summit of Rogers Pass and buried the railway tracks about thirty feet [ten metres] deep. My grandfather called out his crew of 63 men and they set off with torches and shovels to clear the tracks.

"Around midnight, he left the site and hiked about a mile down the line to a watchman's hut to phone in a progress report. He advised the dispatcher in Revelstoke that the tracks would be cleared in another couple of hours, then headed back. When he reached the site, all was in darkness. There were no lights from torches, no sounds of men digging, no sounds at all. Another avalanche had come down and buried everything. Only one man survived. The rest, including my grandfather's younger brother, were buried in the avalanche. It was the worst disaster in the history of the CPR."

Julie is the award-winning author of numerous books for young readers. Her novels include *White Jade Tiger* (winner of the Sheila A. Egoff Children's

Literature Prize, and nominated for both the Canadian Library Association Book of the Year Award and the Silver Birch Award), *Destination Gold* and *The Ghost of Avalanche Mountain*. Among her acclaimed picture books are *The Dragon's Pearl, Emma and the Silk Train, Bear on the Train* and *Whatever You Do, Don't Go Near That Canoe!*

While the events described and some of the characters
in this book may be based on actual historical events
and real people, Kate Cameron is a fictional character
created by the author, and her diary is a work of fiction.

National Library of Canada Cataloguing in Publication Data

Lawson, Julie, 1947-
A ribbon of shining steel : the railway diary of Kate Cameron

(Dear Canada)
ISBN 0-439-98848-9

1. Railroads-Canada-History-19th century-Juvenile fiction.
2. Canadian Pacific Railway Company-History-19th century-
Juvenile fiction. I. Title. II. Series.

PS8573.A933R43 2002   jC813'.54   C2002-900706-2
PZ7.L43828Ri 2002

6 5 4 3 2 1   Printed in Canada   02 03 04 05

The display type was set in Bernhard Modern.
The text was set in Bembo.

Printed in Canada
First printing, May 2002

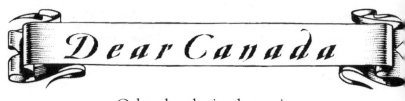

Dear Canada

Other books in the series: